THE MENSCH

THE MENSCH

a novel by

DAVID WEISS

MID-LIST PRESS
MINNEAPOLIS

FIRST SERIES: NOVEL

Mid-List Press
4324-12th Avenue South, Minneapolis, MN 55407-3218

Library of Congress Cataloging-in-Publication Data
Weiss, David, (David F.)
The mensch : a novel / by David Weiss — 1st ed.
      p.   cm.   "First series—novel."
ISBN 0-922811-32-6 (pbk. : alk.paper)
I. Title
PS3573.E4152M46   1998
813'.54—dc21   97-46049   CIP

Printed in the United States of America
00 99 98   5 4 3 2 1

First Edition

Cover Painting: Ben Shahn, *Second Allegory*, 1953, oil on canvas
Collection of the Krannert Art Museum and Kinkead Pavilion,
University of Illinois, Champaign-Urbana
Photo credit: Wilmer Zehr, Zehr Photography, Champaign, Illinois

Bob Kentor, despite, because.

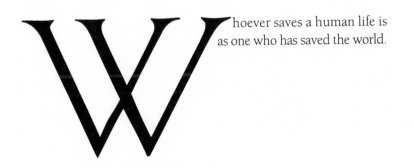

Whoever saves a human life is as one who has saved the world.

L andlord!" barked Leon Roth for the third time. He rapped the door, harder this time, with his key ring. Off the hall's hard walls the word racketed like a rifle report. The vibrations penetrated his chest and made him queasy. Inside, he could hear a TV blaring, Latin music bubbling over. He hooked the keys back onto his belt loop and drummed the door with his fist.

"Landlord!"

1

The glass dot of the peephole dimmed, and Roth thought he could make out an eye darting from side to side as if it saw only an empty hallway. He glanced down at himself to make sure he was visible. Brown jacket over brown pants and boots against brown walls, brownish air: visible. Just barely.

"Landlord," he said.

"What do you want?" It was a gravelly, uncleared voice.

"Mr. Morales?" said Roth, clearing his throat, "you're two months behind in the rent."

"I told your office I don't give them nothing till my stove is fixed."

"I sent the super up last week to take care of that, Mr. Morales."

"Yeah, Gaetana, he came up. But he didn't do nothing. It ain't no better than it was."

The tinny, rhythmic shriek of an infant jabbed through the door. Roth poked a loose tile with his toe. They always broke loose by the doorsill. "All right, Mr. Morales, let me in and I'll take a look at it."

Roth pressed the tile back into place.

"Okay," the voice said. "Okay. Wait a minute. Just wait a minute."

Roth could hear other voices now, chittering, avian. He turned, waiting, and scraped his palm along the craggy, textured wall; mud-dark, originally greenish with a bronze patina, it swallowed most of the light. The glow from the halo-shaped fluorescents in the ceiling was sucked up like an echo. Day and night these lights buzzed like flies spinning around, flat on their backs, in the last stage of dying. In his six years coming here, not one bulb had ever burned out that he could remember—the only things in this building that didn't need replacing. They seemed to have an energy source all their own.

He peered down the hall. Eternity would probably look like this, narrow, dim, no way out. It would take a saint to live here that long. No one else could stand it. No one else should have to, even for part of a lifetime. A saint might even look forward to it;

if you were St. Sebastian with all those arrows through your gut, a place like this might even seem like a blessed relief. Maybe Fein should run an ad in the classifieds: "Apartments for rent—martyrs wanted." Except that ads weren't necessary. With so many buildings in the Bronx torched in these past few years, Fein Realty hardly had a vacancy anywhere. Even a priest would have trouble finding an apartment these days. "Come on, Morales, come on," Roth seethed, toeing the wall. The air hung motionless and chilly as in a cave far below the surface of the earth. It was amazing, he'd only just arrived, and already it felt like months, years. He felt like a stalagmite forming.

Earlier, on the drive down from the office, sunlight had slit open the belly of solid, gray clouds and smeared the buildings along the Grand Concourse with a thick, yellow glaze. Idling at a light on 176th, he'd watched as each brick in the raking sunlight stood out, etched so distinctly that every pit and pebble on its surface made or caught a shadow. Tiny worlds of rich topographic detail, golden-red. Like the earth zoomed in on for a satellite map. So much going on in a space no larger than a billfold which, a moment before, had seemed flat, empty, unworthy of attention.

His eyes throbbed as they did when he fought back his feelings at the heart-wrenching end of some movie or other. Like at *Old Yeller*. That one had really torn him up as a kid. The father raising the long barrel of his gun at the once faithful but now snarling, rabid dog. "Well, son," the father seemed to say in his hokey Western drawl, "you have to kill what you love; otherwise you can't be sure you love it. The only way you'll grow up is to watch what you love die."

Leon hated that the bastards had made him love the dog. The film's arid landscape—or the dog's fur or maybe its eyes—was the same buttery yellow as this unnatural light.

As he nursed his container of coffee waiting for the light to change, Roth had the sensation that something was about to be revealed, like the inside of an amethyst geode whose cocooned crystals he'd often seen in gift shop windows. Someone had tapped on that rough, ordinary surface to crack it open. Someone had known to do that. If the crude and violent earth could forge something so beautiful, however inadvertently.... Roth found himself hoping the light would fall on him, too, like a benediction. His car, however, lay in a building's long shadow. He was always in the shadow of something, it seemed. Then the traffic light had turned green, someone behind him leaned on the horn, and the sun's brilliance withdrew from the sky as suddenly as it appeared.

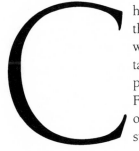heck it out!" said Morales as he led Roth to the kitchen through a living room bright with mirrors. The air was hectic with the tang of fried peppers, Bustélo and salsa. A parrot squawked in a pink onion-dome cage. From the darkness of a half-closed door, an old woman's face peered out. A boy and girl still in pajamas clung to Morales's legs.

Morales turned the knob for the oven. Side by side in the narrow kitchen they listened to the gas hiss.

"See, man, this ain't safe. I got kids here. I don't want them living in no dangerous place."

Roth shut off the gas. He got down on his knees and looked in through the broiler. The pilot light was off. He got out some matches and relit the small, blue flame. He turned the knob; after a moment, the burner came on like a blue rug being rolled out. "It's working, Mr. Morales. Sometimes the pilot goes out, that's all. If it does, you just have to relight it. Let me show you."

"No, man, that stove's not safe. One day, I'm not here, gonna be a big explosion my wife goes to cook something. That stove's broken. I ain't living with no broken stove. I want a new one that works."

Roth turned the knob again and heard the soft whoosh of ignition. The boy and girl were down on all fours with their faces in the broiler door. Heat lifted their bangs. They held out their hands to feel the warm gusts.

"Look, there's nothing wrong with this one," Roth repeated without conviction, the way he said most things. How did salesmen manage it day in and day out, conviction without belief? To feel strongly for no reason. Maybe that was the meaning of self-interest. *The trouble with you, Leon, is that you don't believe in yourself,* was how Magda saw it. *It's even worse than that. You don't believe there's anyone there to believe in. That's what I like about you, Leon. You're attached by the thinnest thread.*

"Hey, you kids! How many times I got to tell you to keep away from there. I catch you near this stove again, I'm going to give it to you but good."

The boy and girl jumped up and went back to clutching Morales's pants. Morales turned back to Roth. He was bleary-eyed and unshaven. His mustache hung raggedly over his mouth. An effluvia of beer and onions came off his breath. "I'm not giving you a cent till something's done about this."

Roth turned the knob and the oven came on.

"You can turn that all you like. The stove don't even cook right."

"What's wrong with the way it cooks?"

"Nothing tastes right that comes out of there. Everything is burned or raw. I get home from work, I want a good meal, not some oven that don't work right. Look at it. It's all banged up."

Morales pointed to the gouges where gray metal showed through the shiny white. An old, perfectly good stove. Roth debated whether to argue with him. The kids began slapping at each other, using Morales's legs as shields. They lunged and giggled, hitting harder and harder. Morales's pants began to slip down his hips.

"Maybe I can get you another one," said Roth. "Not new. But one without the enamel chipped off. I can't promise the pilot's going to be any different. Basically, it's just going to look better."

Roth could see Morales's slight, wiry body begin to unstiffen. He uncrossed his arms and tugged the buckle of his belt. A young woman in a short, tight skirt and a head of exploding orange hair slowed, silently passing by the kitchen. Roth heard the front door click shut. The boy was chasing the girl around his father's knees, squeezing between him and Roth as they went by.

"You make sure it's a good one, otherwise my wife's gonna give me grief. Hey! Cut it out, you kids! What do you think I am, a fire hydrant or something?"

Roth hadn't seen the wife. But he was sure she was there, listening. The infant had quieted. Someone had turned the music down. As Morales led him back out, Roth wanted to ask about the rent again but couldn't bring himself to. Maybe he and Morales had an understanding, and Morales would give the rent to the super. He would tell the office that Morales would pay next week, by the eighth. That would keep them at bay. Otherwise, he would find himself on the receiving end of another of Fein's lectures.

You gotta hondle with these people, Leon. They expect you to. They don't respect you if you don't. Push. If they push back, you push harder. Threaten them with a dispossess. Give it to them if you have to, so they know you're not fooling around. Otherwise, all you're going to get is the run-around.

Roth had often heard Fein over the phone going at it hammer

and tongs with a tenant. Fein kept a list of the names and numbers of recidivists on his bulletin board, and each morning he would work down it systematically, delivering sermons on basic economics, rights and responsibilities.

"Mr. Sanchez, if you don't pay your rent, how can I provide even basic services? Let me explain something to you...." He made sweeping, decisive gestures with his hands which no one but Roth or the secretary ever saw. He spoke as if a failure to pay the rent on time loosened the very foundation stones on which the world was built. He was like a Lubavitcher, like any fundamentalist; no distinctions were made between small and large transgressions. Each offended the spirit of the law. Of course, Fein was shrewdly practical, too. Maybe it was the long history of persecutions that had baked self-interest into the bricks of his being. This hadn't happened with Roth, who envied him. Fein would have maneuvered Morales into a silenced acquiescence.

"Mr. Morales, when you are late with your rent, do I turn off your heat, do I cut off your hot water? Do I?" Even the kids would have stopped playing and cowered behind their father. Fein had wet, bulging eyes that never blinked as he talked at you. They made Roth feel ill, but he couldn't look away. It was like being hypnotized by a snake. Fein might not even have made a concession about the stove. He would have left Morales feeling grateful for the stove he had.

The trouble with you, Leon, is that you want people to be happy, so they'll leave you alone, was Magda's take.

He would switch the stove, Roth decided, with the one in the empty apartment, 2F, which Elvin was going to start painting tomorrow, and hope that Morales would come through before the unpaid rent was caught in the searching glare of Fein's scrutiny.

The orange-haired girl was leaning at the elevator when Roth came out of the apartment. He could see between her stockinged thighs the diamond pattern of tiles in the floor. In the dingy air perfume hung, tropical. One foot tapped electrically. A tiny red purse swung from her shoulder on silver chains. Where were her school books? Roth remembered girls like her from high school, just

9

seven years ago, though it felt like seventy. Walking the halls they were like magnets in those physics class experiments that made all the metal filings move as if with a single mind. This one was like Monica, always sullen and moody, angry at some guy, hard as porcelain. And disdain, she could really dish it out. Guys circled her, on the prowl. She barely gave them the time of day, it seemed. *The thing about Monica,* Magda had explained, *is that she thinks being tough is some sort of philosophy.* Monica copied Leon's homework. He let her cheat on tests; in return, she had let Leon hang around with her. With him, she was soft, weary, confiding. Leon didn't really count, he knew, but that's why they got along. The truth, he used to tell her, was not that boys wouldn't leave her alone but that she didn't want them to. She gave him a weak smile and a touch on the cheek. "You're sweet," she'd said. Soon after that she'd stopped coming to school. Knocked up, someone said. *The thing about Monica,* Magda had said, *is that she thinks her looks are some sort of diploma.*

In the elevator the girl glanced up at Roth. "You got any apartments for rent? I got a friend who's looking, my girlfriend's brother. I noticed one's empty on the second floor." She looked down again. The gold hoops of her earrings swung against her cheeks. There were smaller hoops rocking rapidly inside the larger ones.

"Sorry. That one's already rented," Roth answered.

She tapped the heel of one shoe against the red patent leather toe of the other. "You got something else available?" Her look glanced off his eyes then down to the toe again.

This was a girl who couldn't ask a question without it sounding like an accusation. Roth had something on Burnside, something too large on Tremont, a cellar apartment further up the Concourse. The odor had been unbelievable when the locksmith broke into that one. The old Mick must have been dead a week. No one had missed him. The cops had shut the door behind them and torn the place apart looking for his pot of gold.

"No, I've got nothing. Nothing at the moment," he told her.

She nodded without looking up and shoved her hands further into her jacket pockets, pouting. She had the perfect, full lips for it. A real looker. The elevator door opened at the lobby. Roth watched her ass twitch like castanets as she moved toward the front door. He felt an envy for her simple, musical unhappiness. *Music*, Magda had said, *is the ladder I use to climb out of unhappiness. You, on the other hand, like to wallow in it. That makes you a sentimentalist, Leon.* The door slid shut.

Christ! she'd been beautiful, although Leon wasn't sure he'd thought so then. That he could be so stricken, made to feel so desolate by her! Christ! She'd really had his number. Well, almost anything could make him feel exposed, cast out, beyond the pale. But oh! that glittering, green-eyed sideways look she could throw at him! So lovely when its verdant light let him back inside the charmed circle. Only Magda could do that for him. Or to him.

The elevator stank of urine. He hadn't noticed it before. The second time this week. Roth made a note. The walls were loud with voices. Taki 183. Kool 164. Death 179. Even the window had lately been spray painted: Arc 171.

At the basement, the door jerked open. The platform stopped too high, and Roth had to step down to get out. He made a note. He patted his pockets. Tin of putty and ten penny nails for the super. But no lock. He'd forgotten the lock.

"What have you got there, Edgar?" Roth called out as he approached.

The super was standing in the door of the workroom, holding a kitchen faucet up to the light like an archaeologist examining a new and unfamiliar fossil. His orange jumpsuit made him look like a trained technician. From the day Roth had ceremonially presented it to him, Gaetana had never worn anything else. Roth had taken this for a good sign. Gaetana was Ecuadorean, a small man. Roth had hoped that what he lacked in skill or strength he would make up for in dedication.

"I change washers, but still no working right, Mi'ta Rot'." Gaetana frowned, shaking his head. "Leaking bad."

Schmidt, the old super, would have fixed it as he had fixed most everything. Schmidt had disdained buying anything new or replacing what was still serviceable. He was a patriarchal type— decorous, dismissive and protective by turns. He had huge hands. Roth liked men like that. He had been raised by grandparents; his grandfather had been poured from the same mold as Schmidt. Gruff, naive men scarred in their twenties by the depression. Cautious, suspicious, they wouldn't let anything or anyone fool them again. Ruined men. Hard on the outside, soft-boiled eggs within. *Inside all these for-God-and-country types is an angry person nursing a grievance*, was Magda's read. *If you don't believe me, just consider my dad. Everyone's at fault except him— these days, mostly blacks, the Vietnamese, and me.* Leon had that all's-well-with-the-world feeling around these men, growing up. He'd hover nearby listening to their after-dinner talk out on the sidewalk as they stood in tee-shirts with a hose or broom in their hands, exchanging jokes, grumbling over the day's news, taking things in. They were comforting as wrought iron.

By the open door at the top of the basement stairs, Leon would lie quietly as his grandfather, massive and squat at his desk below, did the books, putting the week's work into the ledger. Mouth clamped on his pipe, burnt-out cigar butt jammed in the bowl. Leon would lie listening to his grandfather's breath leak out slowly through his nose, sucked back in through the mouth, gurgling, viscous, geologic, walled off from panic inside the calm and certainty of numbers. Leon would stare down at the penciled columns, smudged and greasy with meticulousness, with corrections. His grandfather would turn his whole head for a figure and lift it like a length of two-inch brass, following his ruler across the line, and set it down with care not to bung the threads, anchoring the decimal point. He would double-check, and then, totaling the column, the dollars and cents of expertise and exertion would flow seeking their level as though into a reservoir, seven carry the two, his serenity the serenity of a water table, add nine, carry the four, the bills an aqueduct that brought money flowing toward him to catch, to dam. Collect, save, re-use, keep track of, throw nothing away. Nine carry the six. Coffee cans of screws, nuts, washers, bolts, dried-up ball points, dull hacksaw blades, peanut tins of string, rubber bands, hose clamps, wooden shims, used drill bits, gray porch paint, roofing tar, copper coils, iron radiators, pails of old linseed oil, refrigerator tubing, generator windings, half-inch galvanized offsets scraped clean and buffed on a wire wheel, obsolete wrenches, tools for digging, boring. Six, carry the five. He seemed to grow larger as Leon watched, powerful with parts and numbers, impregnable, continuous with the foundation of the house, a stone himself, carry the three.

Invariably, as he came to the end, his grandfather would swivel around and say, "Don't be tapping your foot against the wall like that, Leon. I'm trying to do some work here. Go, why don't you, and see if you can't find some wrestling for us to watch later this evening."

When his grandfather died three years back, Leon had felt like a balloon someone had let go of. Recently, he'd read about a helium balloon with a message inside that had come back to earth thousands of miles from where it had been launched—in Alaska; school children had sent it off, and someone weeks later had returned it with a reply. Leon felt certain it had to pop or drift beyond reach, never to return to earth. Never to be recovered. Like Schmidt. Something had popped in his head. He buckled like a cow hit by a stun gun; it had taken three of them to get him up off the floor. When he didn't die right away, his son stuck him in a nursing home. The thought made Roth wince. He'd only been by once to visit the old super. Schmidt's tongue had writhed inside his mouth, but no words came out. Helpless, he had stroked the old super's obsolete hand. To leave, Roth had had to pry his fingers free of Schmidt's still powerful, clutching grip.

"No good. Need new one," Gaetana said with finality, offering the faucet to Roth with both hands.

It was an old American Standard, solid brass, with an elegant swan's-neck spout. Some tenant must have bought the thing and put it in himself, someone with a proprietary feeling about his apartment. No one felt that way anymore. Roth sighted down the spindle shafts. The brass seats that the washers closed against were pitted. Like a river eroding its banks, the hot water, particularly, had left its mark.

How much water was lost through seepage was hard to tell. Although the building wasn't metered, and it didn't cost Fein Realty a penny, leaks bothered Roth. Not only did faucets and toilets drip, but under the streets, too, the network of old water mains were gushing undetected into the ground. The entire Bronx was ruptured, hemorrhaging. And not just the Bronx. If the city were a person, it would have bled to death by now. In bed at night, unable to sleep, Roth could feel the reservoirs like a giant blood bank, draining away. By force of will he would lie there and try to cauterize the breaks.

"These seats are shot, Edgar. Why didn't you just take them out?"

"This no work," replied Gaetana definitively, holding up the seat remover. "New faucet solve everything."

Roth looked at the faucet again. The inside of each seat was stripped, round instead of square.

Gaetana shook his head. "In much too tight. Nothing get them out."

"We'll see about that. Get a hacksaw, Edgar."

Gaetana sifted through piles of parts and broken tools strewn on the workbench. Nothing remained of Schmidt's carefully maintained supplies. The shelves were empty, the pegboard bare of all but a few hooks. Gaetana rummaged behind a cracked toilet tank and under lidless paint cans, throwing Roth a rueful smile now and then. He would keep searching till told to stop. Roth let him look.

It surprised Roth how much this upset him. His grandfather used to make him straighten used nails he'd collected when Leon had wanted to build something. Whenever he found Leon whimpering in the driveway unable to get them flat, he'd begin rolling the silver dollar in his pocket, end over end, getting worked up for his value-of-a-dollar spiel. *When I was a boy, I. Didn't I teach you the. Don't you know the. Waste not. Haven`t you learned the. Want not. Want not.* He would unbend a few nails, showing Leon how, and go back inside. His grandfather couldn't tell the difference between cheap and frugal. The go-cart he wanted never got built. Or that rocking horse on wheels. Roth made a note. Fein had told him from the start to ride Gaetana's ass. Industriously, Gaetana was searching the same places for the third time. You had to take a stand somewhere. Everything turned to shit otherwise. Magda would play the same notes on the piano over and over like a record stuck in a groove.

Nothing, Leon, is almost indistinguishable from something. Like playing well and playing badly. Only the smallest difference in phrasing keeps them apart. Or like you and me. With us, though, it's impossible to practice. That's really too bad.

"Forget it, Edgar. If it's not here, it's not here," Roth said with weary disgust. He put the notepad in his pocket.

D id you write them down, Edgar?" Roth asked as usual.

On his kitchen table Gaetana had formed small, grimy piles: cash, money orders, welfare checks, personal checks, envelopes with coins inside, some with notes attached. They were about to begin the rent money ritual.

"No is necessario, Mi'ta Rot'. I remember. Um, this is Rosario, 6H. This from Ramirez. And this, this is 1E ... um, Kelly. You know, that old guy with the cats. Oh." Gaetana drew out a smaller wad from his other pocket and counted out five singles, adding it to a pile. "This go with Ramirez's rent. She give me two of her chickens when she pay me. 5F."

Roth marked the amounts down in his notepad. The last stack of bills was held together with a bobby pin. "Who gave you this one, Edgar?"

Gaetana stared at the pile, then at Roth, then at the money again, alert and nervous like a bird that can't decide to take one more peck or fly off.

"Was it Samuel?"

Edgar squinted.

"Zamorro?"

Edgar frowned and shook his head.

"How about Hammersmith, 2C? The guy who vends hot dogs down by the courthouse."

Edgar narrowed his eyes as if he'd caught sight of something far off. "Oh, yeah! I know." A smile mushroomed on Gaetana's face. "Psarch!"

"You mean, Psarcic?"

"The wife. Lots of yelling, things breaking. Estevez tell me. Later, she come down, give me this. Look bad, very bad. Here, here, and here," he said, crossing the kitchen to point at regions on his wife's face. She brushed his hand away as she shifted the receiver to her other ear. Edgar couldn't think of the word and mimed striking his wife's face as she shook her head vigorously into the mouthpiece.

"No slap her. Fist," he said, brandishing his, victorious. "Fist!"

As Gaetana held it there, triumph waning, his wife grabbed his wrist and jabbed the air with it as if he were a boxer who'd just won a split decision. For Roth the triumph was that Gaetana had remembered at all who the money belonged to.

As they waited at the elevator, Gaetana fumbled at an inside pocket of his jumpsuit and handed Roth a square envelope.

"Who's it from, Edgar?"

"Obergon. You know, fourth floor. He give it to me yesterday," said Gaetana. Inside Roth found a get-well card and five crisp hundred-dollar bills.

"You shouldn't have taken this. It's too little too late. They served him with the notice Friday. Unless he's back in court this morning, it's all over for him. You'll have to give it back, Edgar."

Gaetana shrugged.

Obergon. Roth had put the eviction out of his mind. It was set for five p.m. today. Secretly he had hoped Obergon would get a postponement. Roth couldn't imagine him leaving voluntarily; there was bound to be a confrontation. Obergon would refuse to open the door; they would have to break in. Even with the eviction marshal there, and the police, anything might happen. Obergon was volatile, a radioactive substance with a short half-life. He scared Roth.

"I mean, who's he kidding, Edgar? He should have done this months ago when we hit him with the dispossess."

In the crease of the card lay a reefer. In its dark paper, it looked like a long, thin turd. Roth closed the card; he slid it back in its Hallmark envelope. He tucked in the flap then changed his mind and licked it shut; he pushed it toward Gaetana. "Here."

"You want the rent?" Obergon had said to Roth. He'd always been excessively polite to Obergon, and Obergon had been polite back, mockingly polite, mimicking Roth. Thinking of it now, he turned his head as though shielding himself from a blow. Leon had begun apologizing to Obergon for bothering him about the rent. He even began whining that he'd get in trouble with the office if Obergon didn't pay the rent soon; the office wouldn't let it go much longer. He understood, didn't he? And Obergon had apologized with a smirk for the position he was putting Roth in. Roth even thought of paying the rent for Obergon to keep from having to knock on his door again.

"You want the rent?" Obergon said, poking a finger into Roth's sternum. The force had pushed Roth back into the hallway.

"If you have it," Roth said.

Obergon laughed. *"If you have it, if you have it,"* he repeated in falsetto. "Fuck you, faggot!" he said, shutting the door.

Gaetana eyed the envelope as though Roth were handing him a live rodent. "I think maybe it better you give to him, Mi'ta Rot'. Maybe he think I not gave it to you. He kind of an angry guy, that guy. Maybe he understand if you tell him, I don't know. You the boss, Mi'ta Rot'."

The boss. Roth slipped the envelope in beside his notepad.

"Okay, Edgar, I'll take care of it."

"Oh, Mi'ta Rot'? 4G want to see you."

"What about?"

Edgar shrugged.

"Oh, and that lady on the top floor, um, you know, the one with those big knocks," Gaetana put his hands under his breasts and lifted. "6E, top floor. She say she got a leak in her ceiling."

The smell of urine again stabbed Roth in the nose as the door of the elevator slid closed. He'd call to remind Gaetana about it when he got to the hardware store. The super had four boys, one of them could take care of it. On the security mirror a new graffito had appeared. Kill 167. Roth got out at the lobby before he remembered about 4G. He turned and smacked the up button, but the

21

elevator closed and the car went up without him.

It was a spacious lobby, once elegant. The fluted pilasters in the walls, the crenelated cornices, you almost couldn't see them now. He kept only a few bulbs in the chandelier which hung dead center above a kind of tiger lily design in the black and white parquet. But it wasn't just the light that made the architecture seem nonexistent. The arm chairs and sideboard once parked beneath the stained glass window had somehow brought everything into focus. The stained glass window, too, was gone now; it would have spread a warm chromatic light. Tenants, then, used the lobby as an extension of their apartments. They met there, waited for rides, kibitzed while their children tugged at their coats, impatient to get outside. That was before, piece by piece, the furniture was lifted, and the amber, blue and pink panes, probably lily-petaled, too, were shattered. The Gothic arch was filled now with glass of clear wire-mesh. Those mostly Jewish tenants moved north or out of the city altogether. The weak light that came in now was so diffused it made no outline on the floor. The lobby was a no man's land, a space only to cross, made smaller by the floor-to-ceiling mesh cage built around the bank of mail slots beneath the stairway. Roth stared at the cage. It looked like a detention center, but the tenants liked the protection it gave. Peering in, Roth could see several brass flaps hanging open. He pushed at the cage door; it swung in, unlatched. The spring bounced it shut and the entire cage shook: someone had busted the lock again and jimmied the slots. Yesterday had been the first working day of the month. Leon read the names above the open boxes: Olivares, Johnson, Menendez. Why only their flaps? How would someone from the outside know which tenants got welfare checks?

It gave Roth the creeps. It was hard enough to keep out strangers. Roth thought about Obergon and the things no one would tell him about. The hypodermics on the roof. The piss in the elevator. He was from the landlord. No one spoke to him unless they needed something. He might as well be walking around in a Halloween costume. The opened mail flaps looked like teeth missing. To Social Services, everything was potentially a scam. They would be slow to cut new checks. He should probably write letters for these tenants; it might expedite matters. He made a note, jotted down the names.

Roth stood in the cage, enveloped in its hard silence. He found it comforting. Roth preferred the lobby like this. No pretense. No frills. Little to be taken away. And it was warm. The radiator by the window hissed, the rising steam pushing air through the valve. Even as a kid he had felt this way; he liked things unadorned, without disguise. At night, propped on his elbows in bed by the open window, Leon would wait for a sound, a specific one, one like the rumble he could hear beginning now on the stairs near the top floor. Unable to sleep, he would wait for it, wait until the points of his elbows would start to ache. Straining to hear the first tidings of its approach, he would try to make it come by shutting his eyes; he'd send his hearing out like a dandelion seed on a current of air. Still, he'd hear nothing. He would pull all sound toward him, then, like water into an unstoppered drain—an alley cat caterwauling, the air brakes of a bus screeching to a stop, a laugh, the click and scrape of high heels—sifting. Still nothing. After every noise a cloud of silence would puff up and blot it out. A car alarm, a firecracker, would go off, but those, too, were just tricks of silence disguising itself. He could hear silence hiding behind the sounds of the night like a fat man behind the pole of a No Parking sign.

Then, without warning, the silence would grab him and begin tugging. He could feel himself being pulled away, growing smaller the way people did in the side view mirror as you drove off. The silence was a turning black wheel of such enormity that its circumference seemed like a straight line, carrying him away. Suddenly he'd be so far away, the distance he had come so great, that if he spent his life trying he would still not get home. He was lost, irretrievable, an orphan of dark space and silence, infinitesimal inside the black immensity of forever. He never thought to open his eyes.

Then, at last, it would come. A sound he mistook at first for a further blackening of silence, a small pinprick of blackness that became a syringe of sound jabbing through the mask of sound-lessness. Even at its faintest, at its most hallucinatory, he could feel the mania in it. Then it would get larger, louder, a white, hammering roar of sound, blinding, deafening and violent, shoving air and emptiness in front of it, battering the silence back into its magic lantern—the Lexington Avenue El on its way downtown. Leon would open his mouth as the train went by and let it scream for him. It filled the vacuum with convulsions of being. It restored him. It put the sweetness of the privet hedge below his window back in his nose. Iron, hard, it reestablished its sway, put the world back on a solid footing, even if thin as ice. And he would sleep.

The recollection made him want to weep. At the movies he could hardly hold tears back. Maybe he was just too dammed up with them. He hadn't wept for Magda though he had welled with tears when he saw her long black hair snipped off. Leon clenched his jaw and forced these new tears back. It scared him. Once you started crying, where would it stop? You'd have to cry every tear you'd ever held back, for every time you lost a small piece of your life. He cringed at his own fearfulness. He was like a thing of silence. He felt helpless, as he had when the Irish boys up the block wouldn't let him pass unless he gave them money. "Hey, crybaby," they'd say, standing in a circle around him. "What's a matter, crybaby?" Someone would push him in the back and when he turned around to face his tormentor, another would shove him. If he fell into one of them, he got shoved in the chest, "Get offa me! You got cooties! Are you gonna cry, baby?" Sometimes, they would appear out of nowhere and fall in beside him. "We ain't gonna hurt you. There's some guys from Tolentine around the corner waiting for someone like you to come walking by. We're your friends, kid. We don't want to see you get hurt. Whyn't you give us your money and we'll make sure that no one takes it off of you." Leon hated himself for the gratitude that came over him, that much did he want to believe they were befriending him. At the corner they made him stand hidden in a doorway while they pretended to be on the lookout. Then they'd fling him out yelling, "Run! Run!" There was no one in wait, nothing to run from, but Leon ran, anyway, from shame. He could hear them hooting and cackling behind him.

Overhead, the rumble on the stairs now clarified into a stampede of feet. Floor after floor they came, jumping down onto each landing. They passed right above his head and down into the lobby; three boys, one of them balancing a boom box on his shoulder, the volume pushed past its limit, buzzing, breaking up. It bellowed off the hard walls like the El going into the tunnel below the 161st Street Station. The lobby door slammed shut, the echo reverberating off the walls.

Roth let himself out of the cage. He walked up the stairs to the fourth floor to avoid the urine.

Landlord!"

The door to 4G opened a crack. Steam drifted out into the hallway, the almost-sour smell of beans on the boil. An eye peered through the slit. Roth watched the eye sizing him up. In the crepuscular hallway he felt on display as if behind glass, as if he were that small nocturnal deer in the Creatures of Night house at the Bronx Zoo where he and Magda used to go, cutting classes. They would come in out

26

of the wincing sunlight and pad by the bats, the snakes, the sloth and the opossum directly to the small deer. The creature was always down on its haunches, alert, motionless in its miniature wooded habitat, eyes gleaming out yellow and green as if lit from within. They would lean on the rail shoulder to shoulder, and in the dark, carpeted hush grow motionless themselves, watching for the blink of an eye, the twitch of an ear. More than anything else, Leon was aware of the warm pressure of Magda's arm against his. He imagined them Siamese, attached, the blood of awareness pulsing through common veins.

The deer's solitude calmed and horrified him, its fake confines, its deprivations. Leon tucked his head down against the side of Magda's breast. The heated, undeodorized scent from her armpit dizzied him, made their stillness enthralling. The zoo, the house of darkness, Magda's body, were like nesting dolls that drew him toward some inmost doll, a perfect sanctuary, almost too minuscule to detect. He closed his eyes and the faint red glow which lit the black-walled interior came on, it felt like, inside his head. Magda's hand against his ear pressed him closer.

The outer door had banged open then, flooding the house of darkness with light, and hands drummed along the wall. Leon felt the concussions in his lungs.

"Oh, man! Scope it out! Look at 'em! Them bats are just like Batman! Man! Look at them go! Like fighter planes! *Didididididi. Yawm!*"

"Naw, man, those ain't jets. They're fucking vampires. They want to suck your blood. Hey, Vito! Grab Bobby's legs and we'll toss him in. He thinks he's Robin. Hey! Get back here, faggot, these bats want a piece of your ass."

"Get the fuck away from me, you sick motherfucker, before I frag your butt."

Their feet were skipping over the cushioned floor. Leon shut his eyes tighter as they stormed by, waiting for the untroubled quiet to resume.

"Hey! Get a load of this! Lookit here. He's sucking that girl's tittie. Hey! Sink those fangs in good, Batman!"

"Suck her dry, babyface!" a second one yelled, smacking Leon on the back of the head as they slammed through the exit door. Leon jerked his head up but Magda held him there.

"Look at the deer, Leon. It hasn't so much as moved a muscle."

She stared at the creature as if in its stillness it knew the secret of existence. No shame. No judgment. Its electric eyes all-seeing or unseeing. Magda undid the top buttons of her blouse and pulled it back from her breast. The nipple was ocher, upturned. Her breast, like the deer, seemed buoyant in its indifference, defiant in its fullness. Her hand pressed to Leon's ear reached around to the back of his head and, lightly, with cool fingers, drew it down.

"I hate a false accusation, don't you?" Magda had murmured to the deer.

L andlord, Mrs. Bonforty," said Roth, aware the eye was still staring at him through the door. "The super said you wanted to see me about something."

Roth heard chains being slipped off their latches. One. Two. A third. The door opened again. A tall, heavy, black woman with a yellow kerchief knotted on top of her forehead beckoned him in. She was holding an orange in one hand, a spatula in the other.

"Oh, I didn't see it was you, Mr. Roth. You're not wearing your hat today."

"I thought it was going to be warm out."

"Warm? What you consider warm, Mr. Roth? You some kind of Eskimo? What weather report you been watching? Weatherman say snow."

"Well, when the sun came in the window this morning, something about it felt spring-like, I don't know why. Why do I smell wet paint? Are you still using that can I gave you last month?"

"This is what I want to show you about," she said, turning.

Roth followed Mrs. Bonforty's wide aproned hips, ducking under a clothesline in the hall strung with sheets. A game show squealed from the living room—prices, appliances, loud, slow ticking. Sprawled on the couch was a plump girl with hair done up in corn rows. She didn't turn her head. Had it been her unresponsive eyes watching through the crack before her mother opened the door?

The bedroom they entered was quiet and unlit. The room's one window looked out on the brick wall of the adjacent building, an alley's width away, yet the curtains were half-drawn. Perpetual dusk. Roth could make out two beds, one against either white, bare wall. From one bed came shallow, congested breathing. A clammy odor of wet paint and must assaulted his nose. He fought an urge to hold his breath. Mrs. Bonforty led him between the beds over to the outside wall beneath the window and pointed down at the baseboard. "The paint. This is what I want you to see."

Roth knelt down. The wall was wet to the touch and cold. Something came off on his fingers. Plaster. It had begun to soften. The bottom of the wall, as he looked more closely, was blue and green with mold. Along the top of the baseboard, fungus was growing, the kind fanning out from the bark of fallen trees that Roth had always marveled at as a sign of nature's economy and self-renewal.

From the bed a pair of eyes opened and tipped toward him.

The boy stared without blinking. He breathed stertorously as if a man were sitting on his chest. Roth made warmth come into his face as he looked at the boy. He recalled from the late summer a sweet, mischievous grin, a high shrill voice, a front tooth missing. Sickness had taken the intelligence out of the boy's face. Leon smiled to reassure him. The boy just stared.

All but two of the radiator's ribs were cold. Roth tapped the air valve with his wrench. Air whistled out, then stopped. He made a note. "What's the matter with him?"

"He's got croup, the doctor said."

"He doesn't sound so good. I'm not sure this is a good room to keep him in. It's too damp."

"Doctor say he need moisture. Dry is bad. He fight with his sister if I put him in there with her."

Roth looked over at the boy. Under the covers to his neck, he seemed to be all head. He was gazing up at the ceiling now. Roth remembered what it was like to travel the landscape of ceiling cracks, driving their hairpin curves up into imagined mountains. Flat on your back, it was a feverish pleasure, even a kind of freedom. The boy's eyes, though, seemed locked in place, indifferent. Maybe it was too dim to see the ceiling. Air whistled between the boy's cracked lips. His chest rose and fell with effort. Roth followed Mrs. Bonforty out. His own chest had begun to tighten. Roth made a note.

"We'll have to find out why that wall is so wet. Then I'll have the painter redo that room."

In the hall, Roth moved aside a sheet and touched the wall lightly. It, too, was damp. "You may want it humid in here, Mrs. Bonforty, but this is too damp. It's not good for the walls. It can't be that good for the kid."

She nodded. She was still holding the orange in her hand. Roth nodded back. But he didn't really know what her nod meant. The boy's eyes had been like the whites of sunny-side up eggs. Roth felt his gorge rising. Why was it so wet in here? His shirt was sticking to his back. "Is there some other reason it's so damp in here?"

Roth poked his head in the open bathroom. All the faucets were spritzing a thin stream of hot water. A brown discoloration streaked the sink and tub. He leaned in beneath panty hose and blue jeans dripping from the shower rod. He tried the handles. They were shut tight. He twisted the ones in the sink. They, too, were fully shut. Roth turned to Mrs. Bonforty who filled the doorway.

"I'll have the super up to take care of these."

"He's already up here, working."

"He is? Right now?"

Roth followed Mrs. Bonforty to the kitchen. All of her was as solid and rounded as the orange cupped in her palm. What would it be like to have her for a mother? Deep bodily sympathy. A surface firm as the earth. The girl on the couch didn't look up as they passed by. She was painting her nails, the two spread fingers she held up glistening, a wild shade of violet.

In the kitchen, a dank earthy smack like stepping into a greenhouse caught Roth across the face. The windows were fogged. Beads of water jiggled like larvae from the ceiling. The lid on the pot of beans was lifting and dropping loudly as steam puffed out. Next to the pot a bowl mounded high with sliced oranges gleamed like the daughter's iridescent nails and added to the equatorial effect. It all seemed so gay. A carnival of a catastrophe. But the chill of the bedroom and the boy with his heavy, immobile head gave Roth a shiver.

From the sink, hot water was billowing up from the holes where the faucet had been. Mrs. Bonforty had put a pan under the sink to catch the water that ran down, but the pan was overflowing. Towels had been laid down, but already they were sodden, and water was running out onto the linoleum past the tools Gaetana had left scattered in the middle of the floor. Roth crouched and reached in under the sink to put his channel locks on the valve. The water slowed to a quiet bubbling. He emptied the pan, set it back in place, then gathered the tools by the wall.

"Look," said Roth. "The super will be back up here as soon as we get a part for the faucet. It will be as good as new. Try to keep the floor from getting too wet in the meantime, all right?"

Mrs. Bonforty nodded again. In her nod was neither belief nor disbelief. It meant, Leon had come to realize from other conversations, that she had heard his words, and they could mean anything, either something or nothing; she would wait and see. Well, he would make sure Gaetana got back here, posthaste. And why hadn't he come back up to do the washers in the bathroom while he was waiting for the faucet? Mrs. Bonforty pulled a hand from a pocket of her apron. Roth thought for a moment that she was handing him the orange. His gums throbbed at the thought of its stringent taste, but pinched between the orange and her thumb was a folded slip of paper, the rent check.

R oth climbed past the sixth floor to the roof. The bulb was out on the landing. He stopped at the door and felt along the key ring hooked to his pants. The keys were crowded on, and he fumbled through them for the small Masterlock key, #652. Fein had all his padlocks keyed the same. The lock, however, when he reached for it, was missing, the chain dangling. Roth zipped his parka, shoved the door open and stepped out into daylight.

The sky was dull, heavily overcast. Maybe Mrs. Bonforty's weatherman was right. The wind was razory. From where he stood, he could see rooftops in all directions. It was like being up on a mountain top amid a range of mountains. Or what Leon imagined that was like. Not a person in sight in the entire panorama. He got his bearings by the flag on Yankee Stadium and made his way to the parapet on the 162nd Street side. He leaned over the copestone to locate the fire escape on the E line. It was right below him. Further below, he saw Gaetana, looking back over his shoulder, walking south toward 161st, the orange overalls sticking out from under a green jacket. Where in the hell is he going, Roth wondered. The hissing leaks in Bonforty's bathroom made him feel as if something was going wrong in his body. Gaetana passed by the open hood of a gypsy cab, the two men in front of it examining what looked like an air filter. The one with maroon pants Roth recognized as Mrs. Bonforty's man. Thin and bony. Always the same pants. Roth had never seen him in the apartment. Whenever they passed on the street, he appeared angry, in a hurry. He avoided the building when Roth was around, exiled. But he was always on the street working on that car. Roth wondered when he actually drove it. Across the street, double-parked, an oil truck was making a delivery. Leon felt too cold to make a note. A UPS van was idling behind the oil truck. The impatient driver sounded the horn. Across from the van, a window opened and a woman leaned out to yell something at a small boy in a baseball cap who was kicking a ball against the front door; the boy went on kicking anyway. Roth liked this vantage from which he could observe unseen. It was like being in the audience of a play, one without a real plot. Things happened, random, inconsequential, always absorbing, absorbed in themselves, the boy bouncing the ball now, over and over. Sometimes they intersected or added up, sometimes not. He could watch all day. There was Gaetana still, a speck mingling with other specks, just the orange visible. Roth's back felt moist and cold.

35 / THE MENSCH

He worked his way along the parapet wall examining the tar for tears, blisters, cracks. The roof was getting dried out. A coat of tar paint this spring, and maybe they could get away with not repapering for another year. He poked here and there. The roof was littered with beer bottles, more syringes, a small dead bird. He made a note. Bent over, he inched his way along. Wherever he found a split he circled it with a stick of blue chalk that he carried in his bulging pockets.

His lower back was starting to stiffen from stooping; Roth squatted down. There was a ripping sound. *Damn!* He had split his pants down the middle. *Damn!* His pockets were too full. And he was putting on weight. He could feel it every time he buttoned his jeans, fat lipping over his belt. He was out of shape. He puffed walking up stairs now. It wasn't really exercise, taking the steps, though he told himself it was. He was eating too many meals out. All of them, really. He hated eating alone. The soft cacophony of voices from other tables soothed him. It was all the company he needed. It kept him from feeling absurd, self-conscious, superfluous. But when he ate, he ate too much. Gravied mashed potatoes, egg foo yung, smoked ribs—he overate, trying to recapture the pleasure of the first few mouthfuls. He barely chewed. He could tell he was full only when his stomach began to ache, distended. Yes, he had begun to lose his grip on himself. How much secret effort went into convincing yourself, fooling yourself really, that you were still the same. Soon he would be waddling, unable to bend down and tie his shoes. That was coming. He'd fool himself about that too when the time came. He heard the ripping sound again.

In profile against the chimney stack, two people were standing together. The girl was pressed to the brick; the guy had his head buried in her shoulder. "Awgh, girl, you're making me crazy," Roth heard him say. More ripping, her jacket scraping the brick. Leon could see that she had both hands inside his open fly. A pair of red panties slid down her legs; she stepped out with one foot, pushed down his pants. He hiked up her skirt and then lifted her by the ass. She scissored her legs around his hips. The panties swayed from her ankle like a red flag at the end of an oversized load. The guy ground his head into the wall as he jerked her higher a few times. She gave a small cry. He crouched until his knees wedged into the wall. He began to push; soon he was pounding into her, hard, like a jackhammer.

Leon should have yelled at them, told them to get off the roof. Now it was too late, he couldn't move. His legs ached from squatting, and he tipped forward onto his knees. The guy smeared his face across the girl's chest and burrowed it into her lovely, exposed neck. Leon recognized Morales's daughter. She threw back her head to mimic ecstacy the way women did in soda commercials, eyes shut. The guy piledriving her. Morales's daughter opened her eyes, large and brown. In the elevator she couldn't even meet his eye. Now, she gazed directly at Roth. Startled, he was about to get up and back away, but her eyes held him. She wasn't alarmed that he was watching. She seemed not to care. She curled the bright pink nails of her left hand around the back of her guy's neck to keep it there. As she stared at Leon, the girl's mouth began to open. Leon could see the tips of her small white teeth, and then her tongue floating between her lips. She was being jerked up and down more slowly and more powerfully now. Her head began to wobble on her long neck, but she didn't take her eyes off Roth; Leon, on his knees, rocked forward, his hands on his thighs. He was beginning to lose sensation in his feet. Then her eyes lost focus and closed, her legs unclasped, she seemed to go limp as a doll. Her fore-head smashed down on the guy's shoulder as he pummeled into her tirelessly.

Roth made his way down the darkened stairs. His legs felt rubbery, bloodless, not his own, and he leaned heavily on the wall for support. He stopped once and put his hand between his legs to make sure his pants really weren't torn. He didn't know where his legs were taking him. Between the fifth and fourth floors Roth let himself down on a step to rest.

The thing about sex, Leon, is that it's a great excuse for two people to take their clothes off together. Did you ever consider that consummate and consommé might come from the same root? That's something I like about you, Leon. Sometimes you'd just as soon share some hot soup.

That was an amazing thing, the day Magda had come home with him after school. His grandmother was at the doctor's, the house quiet. Leon couldn't recall how they ended up on his bed, obligated, perhaps, by being alone. Magda's warm breath ran like liquid down his neck and cooled like something spilt. Her brown sweater gave off a stale odor of sweat, and Leon held her lightly, stiffly, glancing around his room, wondering what to do next. Nothing came naturally, and Leon lay frozen in position, afraid to break the spell, not sure if there was a spell to break. Together they lay, alert and motionless, like furry animals that sensed a predator near. He felt her chest expand against his and contract, her damp breath pouring out, all other sensation drowned in his own hectic pulse. He was supposed to put his hand under her sweater, he knew, take hold of her breast, get her hot, excited—where had he heard that?—she was probably waiting for him to do something. The more panicky he felt the quieter he got. She lay just as still. Everything he thought of to do seemed artificial, too intentional, like the topless models in the *Playboy* magazines he sometimes bought. What separated him from their tanned, glistening bodies was the way they looked out at him coyly and brazenly under frothed or veiling hair, sure of what he wanted, knowing what they had to do. It was like a dance they'd rehearsed the steps to. They made it seem as if this were exactly what they, too, wanted. He'd actually believed that they could even make their nipples rise and go taut. He didn't know then about the special ice cubes the photographer used on them. Nipples as dark as Magda's birthmark which snaked down beneath her left ear.

He was small, he could tell; he didn't think Magda could feel him against her. A hard-on would have embarrassed him, he didn't know why, as if it would reveal he had only one thing on his mind. Strands of her hair lay across his lips and tickled; he tried to blow them gently off. Her hair was dense, black and oily near the scalp, nondescript as her sweater and worn, brown cords. He was growing warm against her. He had been surprised how hot her palm had felt when she clasped his hand walking to the subway station. She squeezed and he squeezed back, chosen. Before that, they had been, what, friends? She was often talking about things he didn't know or understand. When he and his friends were reading Hesse's *Demian*, Magda was being blown away by *The Glass Bead Game*.

The secret, Leon, she had informed him, *is to realize that everything is a game. We're playing by rules someone made up, and we think that's just the way it is, but, really, it's just a big joke, and the joke's on us. Can't you see that? You're just a pawn till you do.*

And Leon had acted like he did see it. Magda, who saw through everything, couldn't see through him, though, or she saw something about him that he didn't. Maybe she'd liked it that he didn't seem to want to rush things. She had moved first, rolling up onto her knees. Leon imitated her, not knowing what else to do.

"Come on," she coaxed, "let's take off our clothes and see what happens."

That was the first time he remembered seeing that smile. With a kind of shock, he realized it was a smile meant only for him. It seemed to hold nothing back, disarmed and wholehearted. A gift. An invitation. No one had ever looked at Leon like that, so openly. No one had ever believed that he could respond in kind. Yet Magda's look was tinted with challenge. It dared him to be equal to the occasion. He realized that he was smiling back. Side by side, they stripped off their clothes, unself-conscious. Naked, he couldn't believe how beautiful her shoulders were, how smooth and unblemished her skin, how sharp the bones of her hips. Miraculous, her breasts which seemed to emerge seamlessly from her chest. He could feel their softness and weight with his eyes. She was standing right before him, transformed, letting him look, a fairy tale. All the time, this thing of beauty had been there but hidden from sight. How could he not have sensed it? He stroked her arms, the crease of her elbows. Even his hands were astonished. She lay down on his bed and tugged him down on top of her. Rapturous how much of her skin was touching his.

He slid his body over hers. He pushed his pelvis against hers, and Magda opened her legs and hooked her heels around his calves. He could feel the hair between their legs crushed and springy. Between his lips her tongue inched forward like a curious hairless animal. He had never imagined. She rolled over on top of him and he looked out through the canopy of her hair. On the floor of his room, the afternoon sun was spreading languid rectangular shapes that looked like bodies. The shapes undulated as the branches of the sycamore tree swayed beyond the window. Motes of brightened dust arched in the still air, also naked. The air itself was like flesh against his flesh, cool where Magda's wasn't pressed against him. Nothing was the same, or would ever be, Leon felt. He'd had no idea. Fragile, buoyant sounds burbled from sparrows in the tree. Something Leon never knew was in him flew out to join them, jubilant with vertigo.

"Is something the matter here?" Magda had whispered as she reached between his knees. Leon only smiled. She got to her knees and with mock clinical care gingerly lifted his shriveled penis like a slice of squid bait. Leon was surprised how little sensation he had there. Later he would suffer over it, but that first time, somehow, they'd been untroubled, free of expectation.

"This is pretty damn sui generis," Magda had said. Though later he recalled her saying: *"You know, you can be a little too Tantric for your own good, Leon."*

At the third floor, waiting, as Leon came down the stairs, was an old man, his scrawny arms spread wide as though in greeting to some long-lost climber descending from the mountaintop. Like a pterodactyl, he appeared, a desiccated one, something bony and extinct about him, with his arms outstretched that way. Empty skin hung from them like chicken

41

wattle. Cartilage appeared to be pushing through the skin of his nose. Anxiety and glee in equal parts were breaking out of him, too. Lieberman filled Roth with discomfort. What was there to be so avid about, in general? Roth had avoided friendly encounters with him.

"No rest for the weary, Leon. No rest for the weary."

"Hello, Mr. Lieberman." Roth stopped on a step above him and rubbed his knees.

"Just the man I was looking for. Have we got troubles here, Leon! Have you caught a whiff of that elevator?"

Roth nodded. With Lieberman, at least, he could commiserate, there was no blame. It was as though they were united in a common enterprise against degradation. When Gaetana became super, Lieberman had told Leon, dramatically, that he would be his "eyes and ears."

"The sun, Leon! The sun! Did you see it early this morning? Coming back with rolls, I saw quite a show, crossing the Concourse, the sun coming right up out of the ground! Then and there, I thought to myself: This is what it will be like. This is exactly what it will be like!"

"What *what* will be like, Mr. Lieberman?" Roth stared at a tremor in Lieberman's right eyelid. Was it a twitch or a feeling, he wondered, some kind of signal?

"The end, Leon. The end of the world! I thought: Everything will be exactly the same as it appears now. I stopped dead in my tracks. I looked all around. It was extraordinary! But the strange thing was, no one else seemed to see it. No one else stopped to gawk. No one missed a beat. I got a funny feeling then, as though everyone but me was dead. That was why they weren't stopping. They were corpses, ghosts. Oblivious. I must have grabbed myself by the throat, I was so startled. It's still aching a little now." Lieberman grabbed at his throat and began to massage it.

It was astonishing how much play there was in the skin. Roth suppressed an impulse to check his crotch for a torn seam. Instead he sat down. Lieberman sat down beside him. How long, Roth wondered, could Morales's daughter's guy keep it up? It was frigid out there. Obsessively, that first day, he had run his hands lightly over Magda's spine, her buttocks, the backs of her thighs as if sculpting her contours, raising goose bumps. She turned to lie arched across his lap, Pietà-like, soaking in the sunlight of his hypnotic attraction. That such a thing should have happened to him! Even now, sitting on a cold marble step in this weird after-life kind of light, he couldn't get over it. What had made them get dressed? Fear of his grandparents coming home? Or had the moment and the mood dissolved on its own, the doors of percep-tion closing? After that day nothing quite like it ever happened again. Lieberman jumped to his feet and flung out his arms.

"Oy, Leon, Leon!" Lieberman went on. "The things that hap-pen. The things that happen! Today! Today, at the shul, not even a minyan could we make. Betelman fell ill Friday last. Who knows with what. Heart, bowels, gall bladder. At our age, it could be anything. They got him in Montefiore now. I'm going up to see him later, sneak him a little corned beef or something, he shouldn't die of the food there. Without Betelman, we are too few. But the rabbi says, we'll just have to invite God to join us, like a silent bridge partner. After all, if he's here anyway, he may as well play a part." Lieberman lowered himself back down.

"If," replied Roth. "If." With Lieberman, Roth found himself saying things twice. Roth leaned over and rubbed his ankles which were tingling now.

"Frankly, Leon, this is it for Betelman," said Lieberman, launching to his feet. "If he gets out of this alive, his daughter will pack him off to Florida. God's got a long stint ahead of him with us. Or not so long. None of us are spring chickens, not by any stretch of the imagination." Lieberman wiped his long greasy hair straight back. "But that sunlight! That was something. Not to be missed. Puts things in perspective. There, lurking behind the hum-drum, the everyday, Leon, signs and wonders! Who would have guessed!

"So! Leon! You'll come join us for some coffee and a little crumb cake, yes? Bea's heating it up. It's a thing not to be missed, Bea's crumb cake. Take my word for it. Take my word."

"Okay, Mr. Lieberman, okay. I'll be up," said Leon, rising to his feet. They felt more like his own. "But not right now. I have a few things to take care of first. A little later. A little later."

"Ah, Leon! There's no rest for the weary, no rest for the weary!"

"For the wicked, Mr. Lieberman. For the wicked."

Roth caught the elevator at the second floor. A woman with a laundry basket was also going down. His legs were still feeling unsteady. Roth watched his pants to see if the trembling showed. But the woman was paying no attention. She held the basket low like a safety net beneath her rounded belly and gazed at the white sheets as though into a pool of clear water. Not even the sharp odor of the urine which embarrassed Roth to smell in her presence broke in on her. She exuded health the way her small pearl earrings gave off light. Motherhood. It could even happen to Morales's daughter. He tried to imagine Magda pregnant, but he couldn't. He couldn't imagine her washing baby bottles, changing diapers. He couldn't even imagine walking beside her, pushing a stroller through a park, or dandling an infant on her knee, taking pleasure in the sweet idiocies of innocence. Far more than he, she wanted a life, not a family.

You know what a family is, Leon? Forget all those pictures of the Holy Family. A family is like waves at the beach. They just keep crashing down on you until you're sand. A family is an unlicensed looney bin. If you're not crazy to start with, you are when they're done with you. I wish my parents had disappeared when I was little like yours did. You can bet I'd have all kinds of pretty dreams about them. I'd probably even wish they'd come back. It's funny that you don't, Leon. Someone must have shoved the needle pretty far into you.

Roth stared at the woman whose eyes roved over the linen. She seemed turned in, half-smiling, on some untouchable world. The womb was a kind of garden, walled off from bickering and disgust. He wanted to place his hands on this woman's stomach like around a mug of hot coffee on a cold day. He pushed them deeper into his coat pockets.

"Much longer?" he asked.

The woman looked up with pleasurable surprise as if he'd guessed a secret. Her black eyes were as light-giving as the pearls she wore.

"Five weeks. Five weeks and three days, actually."

"That's soon, isn't it?"

"The way he kicks lately, it might be sooner, though."

"No kidding."

"Last night, joking around, Johnny put a teacup with a saucer right on top of him like I was a table or something, you know? And we see this bump come moving across from underneath like a shark. Almost knocked the cup over. 'Get that thing off me,' it was like he was saying. He's going to be feisty, this one."

"Sure, he'll probably knock over everything he gets his hands on and pop his father good."

The elevator jolted to a halt, and the door pulled open, the platform too high. Roth took out his pad. "Watch your step," he said.

The woman gave Roth a nod and a half-smile and went out ahead of him.

Gaetana's wife gestured him inside, but Roth shook his head. "Ésta Edgar aquí ahora?"

Mrs. Gaetana shook her head.

"Dondé fue?"

Mrs. Gaetana shook her head and shrugged.

"Ritorna punto?" Roth asked.

"No sé. No sé," she repeated. With each

question her face grew vaguer, emptier. This is how she would keep the civil guard from dragging them all away. No sé. The blankness of a simple cunning. What was she hiding?

"Okay. Digale, por favor, quatro G. Agua caliente. Mucho importante. Okay?" She brightened. Life returned from the interior. The soldiers were going away. There'd be no interrogation. No one would be hauled off today. For the time being, they were safe. For all their friendliness, the Gaetanas were afraid of him, closed. He wished they were less scared. Or more.

"Okay, Señor Roth, I tell." She lifted her spatula in salute, glorying in her English, then bustled back inside leaving the door ajar.

Roth could smell plantains. He could hear them frying. Did she cut them in strips, he wondered, or into rounds?

In the workroom, Roth called for service on the elevator. No answer. He called the locksmith. No answer. He left a message for the locksmith on his answering machine. He started to call in to the office but remembered Elvin would be there today to start on 2F. Elvin could patch the wall in 4G himself, he decided. It would get done sooner that way. Roth shivered. Maybe Elvin could even help Edgar with the stove. That only left the padlock, no, make that two padlocks, and the hacksaw blade from Jerome Lumber. Some air valves for the radiator in 4G. Once he took care of that, he was out of here. Other buildings needed his attention, too. He checked his notes. What was he forgetting? Even with a notepad, it was so easy to forget.

You were made to forget, Leon. You always expect the worst to happen, but, the fact is, you can't bear the thought of it. This isn't a matter of telling lies, that's what families do. Maybe it's that you don't have enough of one. You're the sort of person who makes explanations that let you off the hook. Me, I like to make the worst happen. That's my problem.

What was he forgetting? The elevator. He went out and knocked again on the super's door.

"Todavía, non ésta," she said apologetically.

"Sus hijos?" Roth asked.

"Escuela," she said apologetically.

Waiting for the elevator, Roth listened to the whine of a spin cycle starting in the laundry room. The heated odor of clothes drying produced an ineffable solace. It lasted only a moment, though. Could one string such moments together into a kind of archipelago? He rode up to the top floor, checked the roof door and found the chain back in place. But no lock. It was meant to appear locked. On the way down he made a note.

Outside, it was starting to snow, though it might have been ashes—dry, gray flakes drifting aimless in the air. Up the block, an ambulance was parked, its red lights flashing. Leon walked toward it to his car. From a doorway at street level a gurney emerged pushed rapidly across the sidewalk by two paramedics. An obese woman in slippers staggered after the gurney with her face tipped to the sky, her hands clenched in her hair. She had on a filmy black dressing gown without sleeves. Luxurious red hair was spilling off the near side of the stretcher. Morales's daughter! Leon saw her face again battered against—was it?—her "girlfriend's brother's" shoulder. He could feel her tongue thick between the points of her teeth as she held his gaze.

More people were swarming out of the doorway. The rear doors of the ambulance were being pulled open. The rich, red head of hair, which he could see up close now, belonged to a wig; brown wisps sprang out at the girl's temples. Mascara ran from the corners of her closed eyes into her ears. This girl seemed even younger than Morales's daughter. Her skin was the smudged ash-gray of the snow clouds parked overhead. He couldn't tell if she was still breathing.

Roth pictured ash or snow falling inside the girl, too, dense and steady, as in a glass paperweight: the girl's head was like a glass globe and inside it Roth could see the girl on a swing going up and back, exhilarated by the feel of snow on her face; but the snow was deepening quickly, and with each pass the swing slowed, plowing into deeper and deeper drifts. Pump, he hissed, pump! Don't let it stop! The girl was kicking forward with all her strength, pulling against the chains, but the swing was stalling anyway, the snow too thick.

Just as the medics were about to lift tne gurney into the ambulance, the fat woman threw herself across the girl's body. Roth looked at the small features on the girl's slack, colorless face. It was like they were shrinking, drawing back inside her; in a minute, it seemed, her face would be blank as a just-born kitten's. Beneath the make-up and the wig was a stranger, some person no one knew, not her mother, maybe not even the girl herself.

The thing about Monica is that she was sold a bill of goods. She should have given it back. Some things own you instead.

It was terrifically hard to become somebody. There were so many ways to pretend to, so many masks to shape your face. Roth wondered if Morales's daughter also wore a wig.

Two men disentangled the fat woman's arms from around the girl and pulled her back; the medics collapsed the stretcher and slid the girl in. Ululating, the ambulance peeled away. The fat woman twisted free and planting herself in the gutter raised her inflated arms to the sky, shrieking—pleading or cursing, Roth couldn't tell which. Two other women came out of the same door. One draped a sweater over the woman's shoulders; they held her as she crumpled against them. A car squealed to a halt, and the woman was maneuvered into the back seat.

Roth got into his car. He revved the engine until the idle held, and laid his head back on the headrest while the motor warmed.

Leon had made the driver turn off the ambulance's flashing lights before they brought her out. They had wanted to carry her down, but when Magda saw the straps she jerked her arms away from them, men in uniforms.

"Let her walk, let her walk," Leon had pleaded.

He held Magda's hand as an attendant walked beside her. She stared at them all with animosity. They went down slowly, slowly as mist. Outside on the stoop, Magda stopped in the brightness. Leon watched her half-focused eyes wander up and down the street. She stared at the crowd that began to gather as if it were a riddle she was trying to figure out. Then she raised her arm, not without dramatic flair, and pointed. "You. And you. And you and you and you," she said as her finger swung from person to person. "How can you? How can you?" she appealed, lifting her arms now in a gesture of supplication. People began to smile, some laughed. A crazy. It wasn't like she was sick or even injured. The paramedics took her by the elbows and led her down the steps.

On the sidewalk, an old black woman wheeling a shopping cart came up to her. The cart was stuffed with soiled shopping bags. The head of a small rheumy-eyed poodle peeped out of one. Leon was struck by the pity in the woman's gray, haggard face. The housekeeper who had taken care of his grandmother in her last crippled years had had the same look. Where did this woman find such sympathy in her own fatigue? "How can we what, honey? Tell me," she'd said. Magda put her forehead on the woman's shoulder.

"How can we let it? How can we let it?" she whispered.

The woman raised her hand to Magda's neck and stroked it. "Youse just one person, girl, one little person. We each just one little person."

Magda let go of Leon's hand and began to cry. Her shoulders heaved. Leon stood there helplessly. Why wasn't it his shoulder? Why this stranger's? He found himself jockeyed out of the way as Magda was hurried into the ambulance.

Early that morning Leon had first found out that Magda hadn't showed up for the start of college. "Some girl's mother called asking if you knew her daughter's whereabouts," his grandfather informed him. "I told the woman you didn't know a thing about it. I told her she ought to keep track of her own daughter, fer christsake. Who does she think you are, the truant officer?"

Leon had immediately driven down from his school in Boston. Magda's parents believed she had been sharing an apartment that summer with some girlfriends, but she and Leon had sublet a brownstone flat together in the Fort Greene section of Brooklyn.

From below, as he knocked loudly on the front door, Leon could hear Magda upstairs playing the piano. He called her name.

He searched the gutter and threw old orange peels at the window, but they bounced off without a sound. The piano faltered on; he could barely make out what it was, she was misplaying so badly—she had been trying to learn something by Chopin that summer, but this didn't sound like it.

After working all day as an office temp, she would come back and immediately set to practice. He never spoke to her then. Her boss was a pig, she hated the job, and she was often in a rage. Leon would sit on the stoop and watch the action on the street, languid with his own after-work fatigue. Listening to her practice the same passages over and over again, he felt that Magda, alone in the room above him trying to make the music sound right, was the image of his soul, though he didn't know what he was trying to get right.

Trying is not the same as repetition. It's about difference. Your koan of the month, Leon, is to make a difference without trying. Try working on that without working on it.

Separate from her, he often felt closest to her. Sometimes walking in their neighborhood, they would slide their arms around each other's waist and feel the unlikeness and immediacy of each other's bodies. They would hurry back to the apartment.

Afterwards, though, it was too much, her openness to him, her searching eyes inches from his own; he felt as though he were being crushed by this intimacy as in a subway car at rush hour. What was being crowded he didn't know, just that there was no breathing room. When had her nearness stopped feeling so miraculous? Leon thought he knew what the trouble was, although it was nothing so grand as one of Magda's Magdaisms: at eighteen, if life wasn't continually intense, he now understood, it seemed fake or faked. She expected too much. From everything. And, the fact was, they spent too much time alone together. Had any of their friends ever come by? The problem could have been something as simple as that.

"I burn hot, Leon, but I'm too small a fire to melt all your ice and snow," Magda had said one night in the dark as they lay side by side, untouching.

Now, though, as he hollered up at her window, he felt that something was really wrong. This wasn't anything by Chopin she was playing; it was doggedly, out of tune and time, a Beatles song, "The Long and Winding Road." Shinnying up the drain pipe, Leon forced a window open. Inside, heat struck his face. It grew hotter as he made for the living room. On the floor, cross-legged at the center of myriad circles of candles, sat Magda. Candles were also burning on top of the piano, on the mantle. The air was shimmery, dissolving with the heat. Wax lay puddled on the floor. He'd never seen anything like it. Magda was rocking back and forth, talking to herself. The hem of her nightgown was blackened and singed. There were blisters on her calves. When she rocked forward the tangles of her long hair sizzled in the flames. "There was a child went forth every day there was a child went forth every day," she murmured in rhythm with her rocking. He stood behind her remembering the news footage of the Vietnamese girl running naked with her arms outspread, a victim of napalm. That day was the first time he'd seen Magda rock that way. He'd seen it again, that summer, when he woke in the small hours. She was sitting on a rug in the moonlight holding the soles of her feet together and flexing her legs like the wings of a butterfly. Terrible things her mother had been saying about Magda to her brother and sister. Frail Hanna, who Leon thought retarded, refused to speak to Magda, shrieking whenever she came near.

"See? Do you see what you're doing to your sister?" her mother had said with satisfaction.

And Magda had rocked that way, seated naked on the bed, the morning he was packing to go off to college.

"You're leaving me, Leon, aren't you? I know it."

"What do you want me to do, not go?"

"Don't lie. You're glad you're going. You can't wait to get away."

"It isn't true," he lied.

"If it's not true, don't go then. Not yet, anyway."

"It's not true, but I have to go. Orientation is starting tomorrow."

"Big deal. So you'll be late. Is that more important than being with me?"

"I have to go. Anyway, you have to leave in two days yourself."

"The world is such a lousy place, Leon. Don't let it be lousy with us. Don't. We've hardly talked to each other in weeks. Stay. Stay a little longer."

"I can't, Magda. Really, I have to go."

"It's over, Leon. I know it. I know it." She began rocking. Shaking her head and rocking.

"I'll call you," he said.

"No, you won't. This is just a convenient way to leave me, that's all. Admit it, Leon, admit it."

"Magda," he said. She shut her eyes and rocked, shutting him out. He watched her go backward and forward. Then he picked up his bags and went out.

"Magda," he again called. She didn't respond or stop rocking.

"Magda?" He began snuffing the candles. There must have been hundreds of them. How had she gotten hold of so many? Leon knocked them over and pressed them into the floor. The soft wax sucked at his shoes. He kicked at them, stamped. Magda kept rocking. Black smoke twined from the snuffed wicks. There seemed no end to the candles.

"Magda?" He touched her shoulder hesitantly as though it might burn him. She was as indifferent as a rock slide. Leon knelt down behind and threw his arms around her to bring her to a halt, but her rocking pulled him along, lifting him onto her back as she came forward. The fevered strength of her body was a shock to him.

"There was a child went forth every day there was a child went forth every day there was a child went forth everyday there was a child went ..." It was like she was whispering an endless string of Hail Marys.

Back and forth they went. Leon had hung on.

Leon rocked forward and opened his eyes. The sidewalk was empty now. He stared at the shiny grease stain where the fat woman had stood. Two locks. Assorted washers. Hacksaw blades. And light bulbs. Better get Miguel to come by with the hand truck to move the stoves around, after all. He made a note. Speak to the tenants in 3A. Radiator valves. The snow was coming down harder now, a wispy line of it collecting along the windshield wiper. It blew off as he pulled away.

R oth shifted the bag of parts to his left arm and knocked on the super's door. He waited, then knocked again. A gawky, leggy teenager opened the door. Shaggy black hair shaded his black eyes like a visor.

"Hello, Carlos, is your father in?"

"Haven't seen him."

"Is he going to be back soon, you think?"

The kid shrugged. He took a bite from a sandwich he had in his hand.

"Well, do me a favor, will you, and take a mop to the elevator. Someone's used the elevator for a bathroom again."

Carlos tore off another bite as if he were eating flesh. "I don't know where he's at."

"Do you know where the mop is?"

"Where it always is, right?"

"Right. In the boiler room."

"He's out helping my uncle."

"The elevator really stinks."

"I think he's going to be back soon."

In the workroom, Roth set the bag on the table. He unscrewed the broken bulb and put in a new one. He could hear from the laundry room the buzz of a washer whose load was out of balance. Leon picked up the faucet. He could feel the water bubbling out of the pipes upstairs. He hoped Mrs. Bonforty had emptied the pan. He pulled out the new hacksaw blade and forced it through the center of the stripped seat. Clamping on a vise grips he picked up off the floor, Roth shoved the blade further in, but the dull teeth slipped, and he mashed his knuckles on the faucet. He slammed the faucet down on the bench. He slammed it again and sucked on his fist. Roth had once killed a rat in a paper bag that way. He didn't know what to do with it. He'd swept it into the bag, trap and all; still, it was managing to move around, to scratch. And it was heavy. He smashed it against a wall. He was afraid to look inside in case it jumped out at him. He smashed it some more, harder with each blow. It filled him with a cold vengeance. He smashed it until the bag split open and the dead rat, its back legs still crushed in the trap, flew out, bleeding from the mouth.

Roth opened the jaws of the vise grips, tightened them and squeezed them shut. He shoved and yanked, shoved and yanked. The blade began to cut. Careful not to mar the threads, he tapped the ruined seats out and looked around for the seat kit he had brought Gaetana last week. It was nowhere to be found.

Maybe Gaetana had brought it up to 4G; anything was possible with that guy. He felt like stuffing Gaetana in a paper bag and swinging him against the wall. Before going upstairs, Roth called the office.

"Fein Realty."

"Ellen? It's Leon."

"Oh, hi, Leon, good thing you called in. Mr. Fein's been waiting for you. There's something important he's got to tell you."

"I'll be in later, tell him. Leave a message for Miguel. I need him at 162nd tomorrow with the carrier. And while he's at it, tell him to bring a trowel and some roofing tar."

"That's what Mr. Fein wants to talk with you about. He wants you to hold back on 162nd Street."

"Well, tell him I'm only doing the necessary. I'll be in around five. Don't forget the message for Miguel. Write it down this time, okay? You know how Allan hates when we forget." Roth clicked off and dialed the locksmith again.

"Hello, Nimrud. Leon Roth. Did you get my message? I've got some mailbox locks that need replacing over at 162nd."

"The animals are at it again, eh, Leon? First and the fifteenth: feeding time at the zoo. I could set my clock by it. You want me to wait a couple of weeks? You could save some dough that way. I told Allan that cage would be a waste of time. See, these creatures want to get into the cage, not out of it."

Leon picked up the faucet from 4G lying beside the phone and fiddled with it. "I'd like you to do it as soon as you can, Jerry. The post office won't deliver if the flaps don't lock."

"What difference does it make? Most of those people can't read anyway. What do they need mail for? They ought to send them back to the islands."

"When can you get to it?"

"Face it, Leon, the Bronx we knew is a thing of the past."

"You're going to be here for the eviction this afternoon. Why not do it before?"

"Can't, Leon, I can't. I think I can get to it tomorrow afternoon. Wednesday morning at the latest."

"Thanks, and Jerry? There's always an apartment waiting for you here if you want it. Don't forget."

"Same to you, sweetheart."

Mrs. Bonforty let him back in. The girl with the corn rows was still spread across the couch, doing her toes now. Not so much as a glance did she give them. That was family life, he imagined. Sometimes, you wished they'd all disappear. He had been spared that. Squeezing past Mrs. Bonforty, Roth breathed in a scent of cumin and detergent. He always breathed in deeply when he passed women on the street, as if by doing so you could gain admittance to their secret life. It was rotten, the feeling of being shut out. He set the faucet down and picked through the tools he'd stacked next to the wall. He peered in under the sink. No box of seats. What had Gaetana done with them? The bowl was full of water, though. He emptied it and set it back in place. The lid was on the pot now, and the contents were simmering. Wisps of steam seeped out from around its edges. Tangs of orange and cinnamon made the glands in Leon's jaw work. He wondered if, down the hall, the boy could smell this or if he was even hungry. Maybe he was sleeping. That would be best. He told Mrs. Bonforty he'd be back.

In the workroom Roth put the spindles back in the faucet and snapped off the light. Maybe he had a seat assortment in the car. The unbalanced washing machine was still buzzing. He hit the up button on the elevator and walked past into the laundry room. A soapy perfumed cleanliness clogged the warm air. No one was there, but all the machines were going. Roth opened the lid of the blaring machine. Sheets with football players on them were tangled up with green-striped towels and a pink bath mat. He redistributed the towels spreading them evenly and turned the machine back on; it smacked rhythmically against the adjacent washer as it picked up speed, but the rinse water drained, and the agitator spun. Roth wiped his hands on his pants and sat down on the bench swiveling the shiny spout of the faucet like the handle of a slot machine, listening to the gratifying noise of work being done.

A woman with black, short-cropped hair and earrings that tinkled like wind chimes had come in and lifted the same lid. She leaned over the machine, peering in. "Boy, this washer's been at it a long time. These things're going to be real clean when they're done."

Roth felt with his eyes the high curve of her arch as her heel lifted out of her pump. "Actually, it stopped at the end of the rinse cycle, the balance was off. It was buzzing a long time, so I came in," Roth blurted out.

The woman turned and looked at the faucet in Roth's hand. He stopped working the spout.

"Are you a plumber or something?"

"I'm the agent for the building."

"Oh yeah, how come I never seen you before? I never seen you, and you're poking at my clothes."

"No clothes. Sheets and towels. The towels are what threw it off."

"You were looking pretty closely. You some kind of pervert or something? Enough crap goes on in this building without some kind of laundry pervert down here feeling people's wash." She closed the lid and the machine started spinning again.

"I've never seen you either," said Leon. "Maybe you just came in here off the street to clean your clothes."

She leaned back against the machine and crossed her arms on her chest. She eyed him closely; the corners of her mouth went up. "Touché, Mr. Agent. We're even."

"Leon. Leon Roth."

"Okay, Leon. Leon Roth. Leon the lion. Leon means lion, right? You a lion, Leon?"

"And who are you, besides having a seven-year-old son?"

"Daughter. And she's only six. I got the sheets on the cheap, Mr. Clothes Pervert. She likes them. She wants to be a football player. I even got her a ball. She likes to tackle. She throws me the ball and then she tries to knock me down. She's a tough little thing. You got to be around here. I want her to knock them all down. It might be the only way. You ever want to be a football player, Leon?"

"No."

"Baseball or basketball player?"

"No."

"You're the type that's probably into tennis or golf. Or squash, I'll bet."

"No."

"Wow, you really are some kind of a pervert. What do you like to do? Make a lot of money, Mr. Landlord? Lord it over us poor Spics?"

Roth watched her watching him. She was only partly taunting him.

"Not money or sports? You must be more than a pervert. What, then?"

Roth picked up the faucet and tightened the cold water handle. "I like to fix things so they won't leak for a while."

She looked at him with detached surprise. "You do that for fun? Boy, you really are a pervert."

"I take walks."

"Walks, too? You're a real live wire. Maybe you shouldn't overdo it, Leon. Too much over-excitement isn't good for a person."

Roth closed the hot water tap as if that would keep the water from pouring onto the floor in 4G. He ought to be going. He could hear the boy's labored breathing. He really hoped the boy had gone to sleep. The woman was looking at him directly as though he were some kind of curiosity. It struck him that she didn't have any make-up on.

"And what exactly do you do for a good time?" he asked.

"Me? Frankly, not much. I'm not exactly in the fast lane these days. I'm kind of pooped when I get home from the lab. My daughter keeps me busy. I like a good movie, I'm a sucker for tearjerkers, I don't know why. I hate that sentimental shit in real life. And driving around in a car, I like that, going into the suburbs to see all those houses with the big lawns I'm never going to live in. You got a big house, Leon? You prune roses or whatever you do to them and use those electric hedge trimmers they got on sale in the paper all the time?"

"I live in a small apartment. Over by the Deegan."

She leaned against the machine as it went into the final phase of the spin cycle. Her breasts vibrated inside her sweater.

Roth stood up.

"No kidding. By the Deegan? Boy, you really are some kind of pervert. To each his own. If you get your kicks fixing little things,

Mr. Landlord, I need some window guards on my window. I called your office, but they didn't do nothing about it. I know that I've got a right to them by law."

"You're Velarde? I told the super to install them. Back in September. He didn't do it?"

"That guy? He doesn't do much, I can tell you."

Roth made a note. "You want to put them in yourself? I'll give them to you. That shouldn't be hard for a football player like yourself."

"You will? All right. I'll be home today. I took the day off so I could take my mother to the doctor this morning. She's been having trouble with her asthma lately."

"I'll bring them up later, Mrs. Velarde."

"Miss. Miss Velarde. Melisandra."

"Melisandra. Melisandra the melodious."

She smiled and uncrossed her arms. "That's right, Leon the lion. You know what they used to call me in school? It wasn't melodious, you can be sure of that. Melisandra the Mouth. I still got a pretty good one when something gets me going. There's a lot to get a person going, I can tell you that."

In the elevator, Roth stepped in a fresh pool of urine. Looking down, he saw in it his sallow, blurry reflection. All glasses and bristly hairs poking out of his nose. He couldn't see the hair on his head. At twenty-five, had his hairline really receded that far? Mr. Potato Head, he looked like. No wonder Morales's daughter hadn't been frightened. What was there to be scared of or attracted to, for that matter? What did Velarde see when she looked at him, a biological oddity? He glanced at himself again. He looked like some one-celled form of life nosing along under a microscope. Eat, excrete. Somehow those organisms propelled themselves forward. And they replicated. Replicated like mad. Reproduction by means of self-division. Meiosis, or was it called mitosis? The idea filled him with disgust. Roth lifted a knee to unstick his scrotum from his thigh. Twins made him nauseous, especially when parents dressed them in identical outfits. Once he saw middle-aged twins slumped side by side in the subway, ankles crossed, fat thighs flopped apart. Same bulgy foreheads and thick black-framed glasses. Each held a pencil in his lap, an American flag waving from the eraser. Worse was the same, sweet, dopey expression each had. He had to switch cars. One of them was enough. One of anybody was enough. People like Allan Fein, molding the world to their own features, stamping it with their urges. Money, influence, children. Fein's five daughters. There had to be better ways to leave your mark.

Fein had often invited him up for dinner when Leon started working. Roth imagined that Fein was already thinking down the road. No sons. Someone was going to have to take care of the business. The money didn't lie in selling but in running the buildings. Income was the thing. Real estate was a depression-proof business, Fein always said. A person would be crazy to sell his buildings unless there was no one to manage them. What could be better than a son-in-law? Leon let Fein think what he liked. Leon thought of the daughters as larvae, distinguishable only by age or perfume, which even the youngest of them, the ten-year-old, wore.

Fein roosted on his daughter's lives as on an egg. Ranged around the dinner table, "Daaad!" or "Oh! Daaaddy!" they whined in exasperation or embarrassment at his remarks when he held forth on city government, spendthrift Democrats or his daughters' hygienic habits.

"Hey, Leon," Fein said, buttering a slab of bread, "you'll never guess what I found the other day."

The girls began to squawk like a fox had come into the henhouse. Fein tore off a bite of crust.

"You give up? A tampon."

More clucks, screeches.

"A *used* tampon. You should have seen this thing. But," and here he scanned the table with pleasure, as if deciding which chicken to take, "you'll never guess where I found the thing, Leon, not in a million years!"

Feathers began flying.

"Oh! you're so gross, Daddy!"

"*I'm* so gross? Me?" Fein fixed the squirmers each in turn. "Leon, I come home the other night, and first thing, as usual, I go over to pay my respects to the parrot, and there, I swear to God, the thing is, swinging from the bird's beak like a bloody pendulum." Leon had never seen Fein quite so gleeful.

"So what happens? The bird opens his beak to squawk hello and the thing drops to the floor. But before anyone can pick it up, the cat comes in and pounces on it and carries it off like it caught a mouse. It hasn't turned up yet. He probably hid the bloody thing in one of your closets, girls. One day, you'll put on a shoe and feel something funny down in the toe."

Fein grinned at them. All the daughters looked remarkably like him. They were like daughters in a fairy tale. Generic. Fein and his brood. He loved them with a proprietary love. Well, everyone thinks his own shit smells good.

A person had to do something. Leave a mark somewhere. Make a difference. A small, useful mark. Magda had gone to Washington, D.C., and shouted the names of dead American GIs through the iron bars in front of the White House.

The trouble is, Leon, we're addicted to gestures and bombs, not just drugs. But not you, Leon. You could use an addiction of some kind.

The world was still coming apart at the seams. Perhaps ministering to a faucet, small in the scale of things, might count. He gripped the faucet's spout like a child's wrist and squeezed it tight. The pool of urine jiggled with the elevator's vibration. He wasn't a do-gooder, but you didn't have to be to do some good. He had never been much good with people. He liked fixing things. When Leon dropped out of college to be nearer to

Magda, his grandfather had put him in touch with Fein. Now it was more than six years. His friends couldn't understand it, working for a landlord.

"Slum lords are assholes," Andy had said, cradling his beer.

"This one keeps his buildings up."

"He's an asshole. He's living off the poor. That makes him a bloodsucker, Leon. He doesn't care about those people. He looks at them and he sees dollar signs."

"So what should he do, give the buildings away? Somebody has to look after them, no matter what."

"You want to know what he should do? He should live in one of his buildings, first of all. Then he should teach the tenants how to run the buildings themselves, give them back control of their lives. Why do you think the Bronx and Brooklyn are going up in flames? Leon, maybe you could get him to try it with one of his buildings. Maybe you could do it for him."

"Listen, this guy's a Republican. He thinks city regulations are a form of communism."

"So he is an asshole. What are you working for an asshole for? I don't get it, Leon."

"He's a responsible asshole, I guess. Some of them aren't."

"You know what Eldridge Cleaver said, if you're not part of the solution, you're part of the …"

"And just what are you doing to save the world?"

"Hey, man, I'm still in school," Andy said turning his clean palms face up. "I'm not just spinning my wheels like some people I know."

Leon had drifted apart from his few friends, though he had recently received a postcard from Andy in L.A. He'd gotten his degree and had gone on to film school. Film was where it was at. Film was the only medium that could capture the insanity of the American experience, Andy had written. Leon threw the card away without bothering to save the address. Neither Andy nor Magda's other friends had come back to see her in the hospital. The day after the ambulance took her away, Leon had waited until Magda's parents left before going up to see her. He had stood beside the bed. An IV bag level with his head was drain-ing a yellow liquid into her arm. The tube seemed to be sucking her vital fluids out. She was white as a lily, deeply sedated; her arms outside the sheet lay limp and stiff like a sleepwalker in a horror film.

"Magda," he called to her.

She rolled her head away from the window and stared at him without expression. It was like looking into the eyes of a fish hauled out of the water. Did she even recognize him? Looking down at her, he had a sensation of vertigo as though he were leaning out over a balcony. She seemed that far away. That was half the attraction of falling, the thought of breaking in on the anonymity of the traffic and pedestrians below, forcing them to take notice of you.

Leon could think of nothing to say. He held out a single flower wrapped in green tissue paper and peeled back the wrap-ping to show her a purple iris, their flower. It vaguely embar-rassed Leon that he and Magda had a flower. Anything "special" always had this effect on him. Flowers, dates, rings, all remained simply objects, things remote from human investment. Why did all the connections between people have to be so painfully senti-mental, so Hallmark?

That's what happens in a consumer society, Leon. People even pay others to express their feelings for them. The fact is, Leon, almost noth-ing corresponds to our feelings.

In the Bronx Botanical Gardens they had once sat on opposite sides of a single open iris and, sharing a joint, imagined a trip down its velvety yellowed throat into a lake between steep, rugged hills: what befell them in that secret, unspoiled place; how they protected it and the animals that lived there; what means of sub-terfuge and ingenuity they employed to disguise its existence from hunters and developers. It was all a great jest, doomed and child-ish from the start, but the impulse behind their collaboration they had taken seriously. Something about it felt binding.

Leon pushed the iris into the space between them. "A token. From the shore of Hidden Lake." The bud was closed; a purple tip poked out from the cocoon of hard green sepals. Leon had wanted an opened bloom, but this was the only iris left in the lobby flower shop.

Her fish eyes went from the bud to Leon to the bud, gaping at each. She stared uncomprehendingly.

"Bed," Magda slurred, turning the palms of her hands up. "Bed, bed of dead, bed of bread, bed of lead, dread of bed, head of ..."

With each phrase her head tossed from side to side. Cobwebs of saliva swung from the corners of her mouth. Leon filled a paper cup with water; he tried to stand the iris in it, but it was too tall. He tried to snap it shorter but the stem only bent. Back and forth he twisted it, but the fibers frayed without breaking. Leon wrenched and pulled until the bud itself broke off and fell to the floor. He had to crawl under the bed to find it. He brushed it off carefully, then polished it against his wrist. Magda had stopped writhing to watch. With elaborate formality, Leon set the bud on the plate of her upturned palm; it was chilled from the cooler, the size and shape of a slug. Magda lifted the bud to her eyes.

"Mud, blood, dud, cud, stud," she slurred, staring cross-eyed at it. When the nurse came in, Magda turned her face to the window.

"Visiting hours are over," chirped the nurse. "Time for your afternoon shot, young lady."

As if taking a pill, Magda spilled the bud into her mouth.

Magda had been right about his wanting to leave her. He was desperate to be alone, to be left alone, to escape her ravenous insight into him. On his own in Boston, however, his claustrophobia vanished. Leon finished out his first term of college and returned home. He didn't know why. Because he was to blame? Because he missed her? Because Magda was a finely tuned mechanism, a kind of seismograph that needed constant calibration? Guilt, love, need, attachment—who could tell them apart? Perhaps Magda could, but Leon couldn't. Indistinguishable from each other, they had kept him steady, made him purposeful. And if neither he nor anyone understood his reasons, it had made them no less orienting.

You have a sacrificial nature, Leon. People who don't know what they want often do, Magda had said.

Leon felt Magda's letter crinkle in his breast pocket when he pushed against it. It had been there for a month. He patted it every now and then like a dirty bandage. He had touched the letter so often it had grown soft, almost as soft as his shirt.

The puddle at his feet with its rounded surface tension looked like a bubble in which Roth could see himself floating, a homunculus in a jar. He looked bad, a failed creation, poorly preserved, gone wrong. The sweet cloying smell of piss put a dull ache behind his forehead.

Small things, then. At least he would fix the faucet. He'd mop this damn elevator himself if he had to. Fein would go crazy if he knew: "Chain of command, Leon! We have a chain of command. What would happen if I decided to run petty errands or make lunch for the girls? Tell me! What? Chaos, that's what!"

Well, small pleasures hid in everything. He felt the heavy cross-shaped handles in his coat pocket; if he didn't have any seats in the tool kit in his car, he would just, for the time being, put the faucet back the way it was.

Outside, snow slapped Roth's face like a wet towel, smearing his glasses. Wind swirled up his pants legs. He bent to hitch up his socks and saw that inches of snow already lay on the ground. He followed the wall up past the fourth-story windows; the brick vanished in a frenzy of whiteness. The storm had come on so

73

suddenly, it felt intentional, willful—the sky descending to blot out the earth, to bury it under flood, only this time with snow. Roth turned up his collar. Already coated with snow, it made his neck wet. Those forty nights and days in the Noah story, they were just somebody's murderous dream; you couldn't erase your mistakes. Nobody ever got to start from scratch. You got to start from desolation, from rubble. You got to clear a little space, that was all, and go forward under the weight of it. He took small, quick, unsteady steps. Maybe this would just turn out to be a squall.

Roth slid into the driver's seat of the battered Chevette Fein had given him for a work car and pulled the door shut to escape the blizzard. The car was often a refuge for him. Late in the day, he would sometimes lower the seat, lock the doors, switch on the radio and lose himself inside Mozart or Loretta Lynn or Lionel Richie, it didn't matter what, until the music was issuing from him as he lip-synched, speaking for him. It hardly mattered that the music didn't correspond to his own feelings. Any feelings would do.

An icy gust drove snow down his neck. The interior of the car was turbulent with snow. He lunged across to crank up the passenger window, but it was up. Pebbles of glass were mixed with snow under his elbow.

"Damn it!" Someone had bashed in the window. "Damn it! Damn it!"

Elbowed on, the radio was crackling, between stations, in perfect tempo with the storm. Snow swarmed Roth's face. He felt invaded, hounded. He grabbed a blanket he kept in the back seat and slammed the passenger door closed on it. Then he fell back into the driver's seat as the weather in the car abated. Only cold air sifted through the woven wool. Roth wiped his glasses on his fly. In his lap the faucet rested like a lap dog, curled up. He remembered the tool kit and felt under the passenger seat for it. Gone. And his Channel Locks, which had belonged to his grandfather, gone too. The teeth had lost their edge, but he preferred to use it anyway, as if it retained something of his grandfather's expertise. Leon felt aided by it, the stains on the blue plastic sheathing like runic smudges the old man had left for him to decipher. How to be a mechanic. How to be a man. How to give off the odor of authority. Roth knew next to nothing about these things. The tool with its predatory diagonals, its force when squeezed, seemed to possess the secret of all three. The horn bleated as Roth pressed his forehead to the wheel groping beneath his own seat, patting and stamping. But the Channel Locks weren't there either.

Roth locked the door when he got out, for all the good it would do. He turned to look south down Walton Avenue, hoping to catch sight of Gaetana's orange legs returning through the snow.

"Come on, Edgar, you son of a bitch, don't hang me up all day," he pleaded. He moved to the middle of the sidewalk and squinted

76

down the block. The street was deserted, oddly rural in its empti-ness. The woods could be quiet, but they were never vacant like this. He turned toward the building to go back in when someone caught him in the shoulder, shoving past, and spun him around. He fell heavily to his knees. Whoever it was didn't turn around but kept walking. A black leather coat. Red-soled sneakers. Heading into the building. That was all Roth could make out.

"Fuck you, too, Jack. Just fucking fuck you," he spit. His right knee was stinging. He picked the faucet off the ground. It had landed on its spout and gotten dented. Some of the silver plating had scraped off; yellowish brass was showing through.

Roth hobbled after the red sneakers into the lobby. Hearing the door open, the leather jacket by the mail cage turned.

"You should look where you're walking, Mr. Roth. You could get hurt if you don't watch out."

"Listen, Velez, you don't pay your rent, you aren't going to be walking around here at all."

"You don't get nothing out of me, Roth, until you replace the bed you broke."

"I told you in court. You give me that broken transom and I'll get it repaired for you."

"That bed was brand new. You ain't going to make it new by gluing it. You broke it. You get me a new one. I got the receipt right here."

Velez took out his wallet and unfolded a slip of paper. He stabbed his forefinger at it. "Two hundred and seventeen dollars and forty-three cents. That's what it cost me, and that's what it's going to cost you. I don't want my nephew sleeping in some bro-ken bed that you broke."

Roth had liked Velez. His square head sat on a tree-trunk of a neck. Simple, brusque, bullish. Velez worked at a meat packing plant in Hunt's Point and supported his mother, his sister and her son. When Velez was fixing up the room for the boy, Roth had Miguel put in a new light fixture in the ceiling. A week later Velez showed him the cracked bed frame. Miguel had stood on the bed to reach the fixture but denied that he had broken it.

In small claims court at the Bronx County Courthouse near-by, they had waited hours on a close, sticky night early in October. Velez sat there beside his mother on the crowded, wooden benches clutching his piece of wood. Leon had gone up and offered to buy a replacement piece from the company that manufactured it, but Velez wouldn't discuss it.

"We'll see what the judge has to say," was all Velez replied.

When they came before the judge, Velez told his story and held up the piece of wood. The judge looked at it.

"What's this?" he asked.

"The wood, your honor. From the bed."

"I know it's a piece of wood. And I can see it's splintered. But so what? You could have picked this up out of the gutter, for all I know. You could have broken it yourself. Do you have any pictures of it? Before? After? Do you have any evidence, Mr. Velez? You say he broke it. Mr. Ortiz here says he didn't. Why should I believe you and not him? Mr. Roth here says he's willing to fix it for you, although he is not obliged to make any restitution. I'd take him up on that offer, Mr. Velez, before he changes his mind."

"Are you saying I'm a liar? They broke my bed!"

"No, I'm not, Mr. Velez. All I'm saying is, legally speaking, you don't have a leg to stand on. Next case!"

Velez stood there, passed by, forgotten. He looked around. A new docket number was being called. Roth moved off with Miguel who was relieved, smiling. He watched Velez after a moment tuck the wood under his arm like a rifle. Roth tried to catch his eye, but Velez stalked back to where his mother was sitting. He took her arm and marched out with her. Roth hadn't seen Velez since.

Roth felt his pants clinging to his leg where he'd fallen in the snow. His glasses had fogged, and he wanted to take them off to wipe them.

"Velez, I'm not going to be able to stop them at the office from starting eviction proceedings. Last week I got them to hold off. But I can't hold them off forever."

"Just let them try it."

"Nobody's going to buy you that bed, Roberto."

"Maybe I'll just deduct it from the rent, Roth."

"They're still going to file if you do that."

"You get me that new footboard and I might just pay you the rent."

"Why don't you just give it to me. I'll have it fixed."

"No way. Who's going to do it, you?"

"One of my supers. A carpenter."

"No good. What if he does a lousy job? I'm stuck with it. No. I'll get it fixed. I'll bring you a bill."

"I won't do it that way."

"Then get me a new one like you said you would."

"That was then. But you didn't take me up on it. I'll still fix it for you."

"Fuck that noise, man. You can wait till hell freezes over before I give you bloodsuckers anything." Velez turned away.

"Look at these fucking mailboxes! Don't you do nothing around here except badger people for the rent?" He kicked open the cage door and felt for his keys.

"Slum lords, goddamn slum lords," he murmured.

Leon stood there while Velez pulled out his mail. He reached inside his coat for a handkerchief.

"How's your mother, Roberto? I haven't seen her lately." Velez thumbed slowly through his mail; he stopped to flip through a catalogue. Leon carefully dried off his glasses. He held them up to the light overhead. He wiped them again. They fogged up each time he put them back on.

"She's sick, man. She's in the hospital. I just came from there."

"I'm sorry. I didn't know."

"Yeah, she's sick." Velez passed out of the enclosure and smacked the elevator button twice.

"She's been sick ever since we was in court. This whole business has made her sick." The elevator door closed. Leon felt the hardness of the tile floor, the unyielding mesh of the cage echoing at him. The starter in the light fixture buzzed.

Roth knocked on the door to 4G. He would reconnect the faucet. Without seats the water would still flow but at least it would go down the drain and not onto the floor. He would stuff a piece of rag down each hole before tightening the spindles down.

"Landlord!" he called. There was no answer. He knocked again and tried the bell. He pressed it harder. No sound came out. He pinched the faucet between his knees and made a note. He could hear the TV, warbling electric organ music. He knocked one more time.

"What do you want," a small, sullen voice said.

"It's the landlord. Can I come in? I'm here to fix the kitchen sink."

"My mother's not home," the voice said.

The couch potato? Leon wondered. It seemed more like a boy's voice, but he wasn't sure. Was the boy able to get out of bed? Even sick, he must have felt that someone had to answer the door. A good kid.

"When is she coming back?"

"I don't know."

"Will you tell her to let the super know she's back, so we can take care of the sink?"

"She tell me, don't open the door for anyone."

"Will you tell her to let the super know?"

"Not even if you know the person, she say. I don't know you, Mister."

"All right, that's all right. You just tell her, okay?" Was he still there? Roth listened intently.

"Okay?" He held his breath and thought he could hear clogged, whistling breaths.

"You get back to bed now, okay?" Leon couldn't remember the boy's name. "And don't worry, your mother will be home soon." Maybe she was visiting someone in the building or when she saw the snow hurried out to do some shopping.

"Okay?" Roth repeated. "Okay?"

The G line of apartments was next to the stairs. Roth sat on a step; he propped the faucet against the iron rail and rubbed his knee. The pants were slightly abraded. The knee, too, it felt like. He yanked his shirttail out of his pants and buffed his glasses once more. He put them back on and stared down the hallway. The doors were painted black. All shut. They looked like coffins stood on end. He spent a lot of time on the outside of doors, knocking, calling, waiting, listening for footsteps or deadbolts to open, shouting through them.

"Magda," he had whispered, unable to knock. "It's Leon." He pressed his face into the crack of her bedroom door and closed his eyes.

"Magda? Are you there?" He heard her breathing opposite his mouth on the other side of the door.

"It's me, Leon," he whispered again.

"Leon? I don't know any Leon. Go away."

"Magda, it's Leon. Your mother wouldn't let me see you."

"I knew a Leon once. Yes, there was a Leon, a was-Leon."

He could tell she was pressed against the door, too. The latch rattled while they talked. He could feel her body through it.

"Let me in, will you? Your mother is watching from the stairs."

"I can't."

"Why not?"

"There isn't time. I'm busy. Go away."

"What are you doing?"

"I can't tell you. I can't tell anyone."

"But why?"

"It's a secret."

"You can tell me." Leon could sense Magda's mother watching him from the landing, her arms strapped across her sunken chest, apprehensive, furious.

When she found out that he and Magda had lived together that summer, she refused to let Leon see her after she came home from the hospital.

"Before you she was just a normal girl. She went to school. She went to church. I wish to God the two of you had never met. Better you should never have been born than to do what you did to my daughter. You! You!" she spluttered unable to find the right curse. "Don't ever call here again." She hung up.

Leon didn't, at first. Then, occasionally, he would dial her number hoping that Magda would pick up. Then more than occasionally. When he started working for Fein, he'd call each evening at different times. He'd come back to his decrepit apartment worn out from the combat and contention, the endless attention to minutiae, his pockets sharp with screws and bolts, his mind vacant. He never identified with his job, at least in the way that Fein had hoped he would. At the day's end, he felt like a marionette whose strings had been set down. Repetitively, absently, he'd dial without lifting up the receiver, summoning the will to make the call.

One evening Magda's mother had called him. "I want you to come talk to her," she had said without even a hello.

"Has she asked to see me?" said Leon without hesitation, no longer exhausted. He'd been waiting for this all along, he realized. This was what his patience had been about.

"No, she asks for nobody, for nothing. She doesn't eat. She wanders the house like a ghost. All she does is play with her sister and brother. She tells them stories. To them, she's normal. But she never goes outside. She never looks out a window or calls anyone. She laughs, though, a crazy laugh, it makes me want to slap her face. All day she moves about the house shaking her head, smoking like a chimney, arguing with God knows who. I can't get a word out of her. It's all I can do to get her to bathe. I blame you for this. You want to see her? Come undo some of the damage you've done."

He came.

"Go away, was-Leon. There is so much work to be done. So much I have to do. I can't keep them back. The latch won't hold. Then they'll be through. I … can't … seem … to get it … to hold."

"Hold who back, Magda?" He could sense her mouth moving inches from his. Her talk, the struggling tone, was making him feverish, dizzy. He imagined her like a go-go dancer writhing in a spotlit cage, forced to go through the motions.

"They yell, they curse at me, they call me names. But it's not enough. It's never enough. They spit on me, they kick me. I make them beat me. Beat me! Go on, beat me! I say to them. It's the only way. The only way I can keep them here. But I can't … get … the latch to … hold. I can't … keep … them in here … I can't." She sounded furious, thwarted, exhausted, far away.

"Who? *Who* is doing this to you?" Leon was whining with incomprehension. The mother was still watching him with a frightening intensity. He felt like bait. She didn't want anything to be wrong. Magda's trouble was Leon, it was that simple. He didn't mind being the scapegoat. He accepted it. He was almost flattered by her mother's blame. But something was the matter with Magda, and it didn't have to do with him. He felt excluded. He glanced over again. Magda's mother seemed to have come closer now without moving, a trick mothers had. He put his lips against the door to keep from being overheard. "*Who,* Magda? Who's doing this?"

"You know, don't pretend you don't! Sometimes they even burn me. They burn me with matches and cigarettes. But I have to let them, so they won't hurt anyone else. I won't let them hurt anyone else. I won't. I won't. I won't."

There was a funny odor. Just thinking about it now in the empty hallway, he could smell it. Like an appliance overheating, but worse. Leon had started twisting the doorknob, but it was locked. He began to jerk the door in and out.

"Let me in, Magda, let me in." He tried to sound forceful, but it came out like begging.

He had never told anyone about the candles. He didn't want them to think she was crazy. Before he had dialed 911, he had aired out the place, scraped up as much wax as he could. He had finally dragged Magda to the bedroom where she curled herself up on the bed. She looked small, shriveled, like a dead spider, though soon she had been up rocking again.

Leon threw himself at the door.

"Go away, whoever you are. Go away. You're going to wreck everything! Stop it! Stop it! Terrible things are being done. Will you go away, please? I know what I'm doing. Please, go, Leon, go! Please."

When the door finally gave way, Leon gagged on the stench. There she was, crouched on the floor, naked, emaciated. Black marks covered her stomach and legs, dotted her arms, her breasts. Some of the marks were fresh, some of the scabs were oozing.

"Oh, Jesus! Oh, Jesus!" her mother shrieked. "She's insane! She's insane!"

Leon slapped the cigarette from her hand. He tried raising her off the floor without touching any of the sores.

"You're ruining it, you're ruining it!" Magda shrieked back. "You don't know what you're doing! Now you've done it! Now I'll never be able to fix it. It'll be too late! Let me go! I hate you! I hate you!"

Leon couldn't tell if she meant him or her mother.

No rest for the weary, Leon, no rest for the weary."

Leon put on his glasses. Mr. Lieberman was standing in his open doorway. He lived in 4C, opposite Mrs. Bonforty. The little chandelier in the vestibule twinkled over his shoulder. Its light fell on Leon like a warm slab of granite.

86

Shouts reverberated up the stairwell. A door slammed.

"You should knock, Leon, knock. I'm not a mind reader. But something told me to open the door and take just a peek. Even my poorest chair is more comfortable than that step. Come."

Lieberman backed into the apartment and beckoned with his hand as if coaxing a circus animal into its cage. Roth followed the hand through the doorway and into the dining room.

"Sit down, Leon, sit down. Take a load off. Bea! Mr. Roth has come. Good as his word," exclaimed Lieberman, going into their bedroom.

It was a small apartment; the C line was all one bedrooms. But this one was even smaller. Newspapers and magazines lined the walls from floor to ceiling and alternated with columns of grocery bags piled on one another, stuffed with Roth couldn't tell what, more grocery bags, maybe. Boxes balanced on the radiators four and five high like barricades. It was like the inside of one of those tombs where the dead were buried with all their possessions, only here it was warmer. Venetian blinds blocked all light from the windows. They hadn't been dusted in who knew how many years, and the cracked, peeling walls hadn't been repainted for what looked like decades. Their lease entitled them to a paint job every three years. Leon would bring it to their attention. Lieberman came back out.

"Let me just put some water on for the coffee. Bea is doing her neck exercises. She will get the crumb cake ready when she's finished. Prevention, prevention, all those ounces of it, and the neck still goes." He snapped his fingers twice.

"Pinch, pinch! Like that and the poor, old girl is as stiff as a mannequin. Well, Bea won't go out anymore. And what kind of exercise is this slow nodding and rotating of the head. Get out, I tell her. Walk. Walk! But does she listen? Bea has always done things her way. My own true love is that woman, but stubborn."

Lieberman emerged from the kitchen with a paper bag. He pulled out a lump wrapped in wax paper which he unfolded and set down on a plate in front of Leon.

"Eat, Leon, eat! This I bought for Betelman on my way to the hospital. It's pastrami, lean. With Thousand Island. Don't neglect the pickle. I've got to tell you, Leon, he didn't look so good, Betelman. Well, to tell the truth, he never looked too good; he was an accountant. All the time it was like he had heartburn. Like everything was costing him, and what was he getting for it? But this was different. Oy! Did you catch a whiff of that elevator today, Leon?" Lieberman jumped up; the kettle was beginning to whistle.

"Bea!" he called.

Leon stared at the sandwich. He was cradling the faucet in his lap. It lay quietly like an injured animal. The cut face of the pastrami looked like an ugly wound. Lieberman returned with saucers. He returned with cups. He returned with spoons and with sugar. With napkins.

"I'll tell you what was different. Poor Betelman. They have him wired up to every conceivable machine, inconceivable ones, too. It looks like a television studio in there. He sees me. I don't even offer him the sandwich, he's beyond the help of any sandwich. He's got the look of a milk cow, but not so calm. And he says, 'Lieberman, what's happened to me. What's happened to me!' But it's not a question he's asking. It's a statement. Leon! Betelman's no stupid man. All right, a little meshuggah, maybe, like the rest of us, for staying in the Bronx; but he's not dumb. Suddenly, it's like he never expected anything like this to happen. Well, it's a terrible thing. But who did he think he was, one of the angels of God? Leon. Leon! Is this what happens? You know, you have knowledge, because you're not the first generation to tread the earth after all. You see, your eyes are open in your head, and then one day it happens, and you're astonished and bewildered like you were born yesterday. Leon, how can you enjoy your coffee with that thing in your lap?" Lieberman jumped up. The oven door slammed with a rattle of pans.

"Bea!" Lieberman came out of the kitchen and went down the hall. The bedroom door clicked shut, gently.

Leon pushed the sandwich away. He hadn't been able to lift Magda from the floor. So many burns, it was hard to touch her. She had squirmed away and cowered against a wall. He had seen photographs like that. Prison camps. Magda's mother had pushed him from the room and down the stairs.

"Go!" she screamed. "Go! There's nothing you can do here. Don't come back. Don't call. Don't think we didn't know it was you, torturing us with those calls."

Lieberman returned.

"My wife is indisposed, I'm sorry to say. The neck isn't responding so well. She sends her apologies."

Lieberman went to the window and reached for a box above his head. The apartment smelled of baking cardboard.

"Tell me, Leon. You must be married, a good-looking fella like yourself." He set the opened box on the chair and pushed aside the tissue paper. Scarves. Lieberman unfurled one. Gaudy paisley design, reds, blues, purples.

"Leon, you're married?"

"No, Mr. Lieberman, I'm not." Lieberman spread the scarf over the back of his chair. With a magician's flourish, he pulled out another one, a yellow and black check.

"Then, you have a girlfriend. I want you to have one of these. They're just sitting here going to waste. I was a haberdasher, Mr. Roth. In the business for forty years." He pulled out another one, the size of a shawl, forest green with flecks of gold.

"For your girlfriend. You have a girlfriend, right? A fella like you, you probably have a fistful." Lieberman drew out another, this one striped, each stripe a different shade of pink.

"No, I don't. I did. Not anymore."

The saucer under Leon's coffee cup had fine lines of green and gold interrupted by a delicate pattern of rosebuds. Leon turned the saucer with his fingers, counting the buds, the minute green petals below them, microscopically serrate.

Lieberman pulled out a polka dot, black and white, and one with rectangles, orange, black and chartreuse. He showed Leon both sides, like a matador showing the bull his cape.

"So you broke up with her, is that it?... Oh, I see, she broke up with you. Well, you'll take a scarf for the next one. They're probably waiting in line." Lieberman drew out scarf after scarf.

He draped them over boxes, over chairs, wedged them by a corner into the piled newspapers. Leon sat turning the saucer. The box was still half-full but Lieberman came to a halt.

"I can see this is a sore point with you, Leon. Forgive me. Take one, then, for the girl that left you. For when you get her back."

"Mr. Lieberman," interrupted Roth. He hoped Lieberman wouldn't notice the uneaten sandwich. "Is there anything in particular you wanted to see me about?"

"Ah, I see," said Lieberman, sitting down. "I see. I see." He began expertly folding a fringed, beige scarf.

"Well, Leon, take one for her anyway. Please. You know, I took one with me up to Betelman. I thought, here's a man who never gives a gift. I'll give it to him to give to his wife. Won't she be surprised! But Betelman, he falls asleep right in the middle I'm telling him how wonderful Florida will be. So I take out the scarf, put it around his neck and tie an ascot. A big, puffy, flowery one. I took pains with it. Like with a customer. And him with a tube up his nose, all that equipment going. I felt foolish, afraid a nurse would walk in and ask what in God's name I was doing. But, you know, it helped. It really helped. To see Betelman looking for the first time in his life like a man of the world, a big spender."

Lieberman jumped up. "The crumb cake! I forgot! Bea!" he hollered. "Not to worry, my love. I will bring you a piece and the coffee just the way you like it."

Leon shifted the faucet on his lap. What was the secret, he wondered. For how long were they married? Forty, fifty years? What would that be like? He looked at the roses on his saucer. Were they fifty years old, too? The precision of the petals, their unfaded rosiness, the exact green leaves, even thorns if you strained your eyes. Each cluster of roses, as he turned the saucer with his thumbs, identical, fresh. China didn't so much age as chip, break. It made his eyes throb. He looked around at the stacks of sallow newsprint. How many murders, federal budgets, housing projects, wars, demonstrations, Supreme Court decisions, box scores had cascaded over Lieberman and his wife without touching them in their mutual devotion? He had seen the wife, back in the summer, walking on his arm, tall and gangly as a stork, hanging over him with a wan, distracted smile as Lieberman, stopping every few steps, gesticulated with his free hand, a one-man Yiddish opera. Now they were burying themselves alive, bricked in together by old news. What could that possibly be like: to be yourself, in your element, only in the presence of someone else? Leon's grandparents had chafed, collapsing toward each other from need and incapacity like crumbling gravestones. Vets coming back from the war, he'd read, were like that too; they weren't able to adjust. They dreamed of the war, relived it. It crippled and haunted them. They were married, roped to it. And that man Roth had read about in the obits the other day, the one who had pioneered egg farming upstate. A hundred thousand layers under a single roof. He'd come to America after the war, worked hard, scraped up enough bucks to start out. He'd been in the concentration camps, it said. A modern facility. He'd had the idea from the start. Everything controlled and conveyered—food, light, heat, eggs and birdlime. He'd learned from experience. The chickens spent their lives in a space no larger than twice the size of their bodies. He drove a truck for the Nazis, it said. Maybe that was it. Everything you touched stuck to you. And you stuck to it whether you knew it or not. Who would he be without Magda to wait for? The building felt like a giant tumor in his gut. So even when you were alone you weren't alone. It all came along with you.

"I'll be one second, Bea!" he heard Lieberman, with a clatter of silverware, announce. "I'm just letting it cool. Too hot and it could hurt on the way down."

How much Lieberman wanted to please her. Roth could hear it in his voice. To please. It was childish, like magic, a password. Please. If he could please her it meant everything would be okay. You feed him his meat, and the world-beast goes back into his hole. Otherwise you have to pray. If you have to pray, then it's already too late. You've ruined everything. It's out of your hands. It won't help then to brick up the door like it's a Pharaoh's tomb. Eventually, everything will be broken into, smashed or taken away. Leon had neither pleased nor prayed. Were pleasure and prayer all there were, all you could do?

"Here we go, my dear," he heard Lieberman say. "Can you raise your head up a little? I'll slip another pillow under. The cake is fresh, very fresh. Can you sit up a little more? Try, darling, try. It'll do you good."

Leon wondered if Lieberman and his wife even noticed the boxes and the papers anymore. Painting the apartment for them would be out of the question.

On the second floor, Leon smelled paint, oil-base. The door to 2F was open. He went in, following the familiar sounds. Elvin was up on a ladder in the kitchen, red bandanna on his head, scraping blistered paint off the ceiling. He expelled a hoarse rendition of "Amazing Grace." It sounded like air being let out of a tire.

"Afternoon, Mr. Roth."

"I thought you weren't coming till tomorrow, Elvin."

"We's cooking today, Leon, cooking with gas. I got my nephew finishing up the windows at 187th."

"I thought he wasn't working with you anymore."

"We got that straightened out, Mr. Fein and me. Vernal gonna work just on the vacant apartments. I'll take care of the repainting." He probed a crack in the plaster with his putty knife. Elvin was meticulous. Day in and day out he painted apartments for Fein. Trouble spots troubled him. He gave each one its proper due. Roth had once seen a Buddhist monk kneeling on the sidewalk cutting the grass along its edge with a small scissors, a blade or two at a time. Baptists and Buddhists both made the small things important.

"That's terrific news, Elvin."

"Yes sir, I got him living with me now. He'll be okay, we just keep him out of harm's way. He's a good boy. I'll have him over here sometime in the morning, if it don't snow all night." He moved off the ladder onto the sink.

"Lord, it's coming down as thick as the salt my granddaddy down in South Carolina used to shake on his corn. Lived to be ninety, too. Good living do that for you. You hear birds when you wake up, owls when you sleep, salt ain't gonna kill you, don't care what the doctors say.

"Lookit here, Leon. See this water stain up where the wall and ceiling meet? It's still wet. You best have a look upstairs before we paint that. Paint'll come right back off. I'll have Vernal do this room last. Oh, yeah, they looking for you, Leon, over at the office. Miss Ellen, she had a real edge in her voice like someone done stropped it good and sharp for her."

"I'll bet. Wasn't me that stropped it this time. Who let you in here, by the way?"

"You know, that little Spanish guy in the orange space suit. I ran into him downstairs."

It was after eleven now. Leon arranged to show Elvin the wall in 4G before he left for Burnside Avenue. He took the elevator to the basement. Two boys fell silent when Leon got in. Purple berets. Black leather jackets. One was wearing reflector shades. The other, lizard skin boots. Fork combs in their hair. They were twelve, maybe thirteen, Leon guessed. They looked as though they'd been playing dress-up in someone's closet. They caught each other's eyes and smirked, glancing over at Leon. It made him uncomfortable. He looked straight ahead.

Back in November, Roth had gone into a building adjoining the one he managed on 173rd street, looking for the super. The rear courtyard was mounded high with refuse—mattresses and refrigerators, mostly—and, lately, sacks of garbage; it stank, and he was worried that it would burn and take his building with it. Once he was inside, it was clear the building was being abandoned by the owner. The lamp in the lobby had no bulb; glass glittered dully on the marble floor. The elevator door hung half-hinged. The mailbox doors had all been pried off. The air was drafty, cold. A child, a boy, no more than five, was pacing a tight circle following some design at his feet. He waved a car antenna in his hand, and he whipped the ground as he went. "Don't know," he said. "Don't know," he kept saying to all Roth's questions, in time with his footsteps. "What's your name?" Roth finally asked. "Don't know," the boy said without stopping. "Don't know. Don't know."

Roth knocked on doors. A woman's voice had yelled out from behind one, "I done gave you the check yesterday. You give me back my hot water!"

I should get out of here, he remembered thinking. In the hard, cavernous silence Leon heard something he couldn't figure out, an incongruous sound like a sea wave drawing back down the beach. He'd followed it up the stairs. On the third floor, it was loud, more like a waterfall than a wave. He walked along the hall and found a door standing open. He knocked. "Anyone home?" he called ludicrously. Inside, it was dank, water dripped from the walls and ceiling. Steam was shooting up from pipes in the floor. The radiators had been uncoupled, and all the plumbing ripped out. Shit filled the toilet and the tub. Leon hurried back out.

About to leave, he heard another sound further up the stairs, a hum like that of a high voltage cable. Apartment doors stood open on each floor. Electric cords ran from the hall light fixtures into some doorways. The hum he heard had become a high-tension wire buzz by the time Leon reached the top floor. Leon had once heard a record of Tibetans chanting. This, he imagined, was like an entire stadium of monks. Excrement and fast-food wrappers crusted the floor along the walls. A worse stench made Leon hold the neck of his sweater in front of his nose. Half-way up the half-flight to the roof, he caught sight of a man resting on the staircase. He seemed both calm and in the throes of some awful convulsion.

Leon called out through his sweater in a muffled voice, "Hey, excuse me, Mister, are you all right?" He drew closer, squinting into the dark, and the man seemed to stand up and become enormous. Leon worked his flashlight out of his pocket and shined it up the stairs. He had never seen so many flies. The man was alive with flies. He was sitting on a step with a syringe jabbed into his arm. His back was against the wall and his chin was against his chest. His mouth hung open and his cheeks were seething in and out as if he were breathing laboriously. Flies swarmed out from between his lips. He was glazed with them, shiny in the beam of the flashlight. On the man's head, at a rakish angle, sat a purple beret like the ones these boys were wearing. Beneath it the man's eyes blinked and twitched with flies. For some reason, the flies weren't lighting on the beret. A kind of miracle. Miracles were stupid like this one. That's what he had been brought up there to see: something remarkable, disgusting and inexplicable. Magda had once taken Leon to her church in Brooklyn on Christmas Eve. The choir, the rotundities of the organ, the stained glass, the pews packed with amens. That was about a miracle, too. But it was about the staging of a miracle. This was something else entirely. This was the real thing. Leon's skin itched. He slapped himself as he slowly backed down the hall, his eyes fixed on the beret.

The two boys got out at the lobby, and when the door slid closed Leon could hear an eruption of laughter. He looked down at himself. He was holding the faucet against his belt. The spout stood out from his body like a giant pecker. Same erect angle, too. He pushed it over to the side. He glanced up at the mirror to see how that looked. A new graffito was sprawled across it in red. Blade 158. He looked down again. He was standing in half-dried urine.

L eon tapped on the super's door with the faucet. Mrs. Gaetana opened it. She held a mop in her hand. A big smile bloomed on her face.

"Mi marito here!" she said, pointing directly down as if her husband were right there at her feet.

"Good," said Leon. "Dondé?"

She cradled the mop and made a growling noise. She pretended to be squeezing something large between her hands.

"He's doing the trash?" asked Leon.

She nodded her head with vigor and briskly shut the door. Leon went out the side door into the snow-filled courtyard.

In the compactor room, as he shook off the snow, Leon watched the super and two of his sons wrestling with a shiny black cylinder of sheathed garbage, fat and long as a sewer pipe. They had their arms around it, trying to lift it off the ground onto a hand truck that was lying on its side. Gaetana had one end raised and with his foot was trying to drag the hand truck underneath it. The warm, fetid air made Leon woozy. They inched the tube over the footplate of the reclining carrier. Lift, lurch, drop; lift, lurch, drop, until it was on. Gaetana braced his back against it as his boys heaved the thing up by the handles. He turned and hugged the sagging column of trash to keep it from tipping sideways and smiled triumphantly at Roth who he just then caught sight of by the door. It was a simple, guileless smile. A smile of effort and accomplishment. As he smiled, the bag split in the middle and collapsed in two taking Gaetana with it. Garbage spilled out on the floor, Gaetana on top. He jumped up, dismay and disgust fighting in his face for the upper hand as he wiped a slime of what looked to be banana and steak fat off his shirt. His sons continued to hold upright the now empty hand truck. Roth walked toward them, and Gaetana began yelling at the boys for not holding the truck steady. Beside the compactor lay another split sack. They had tried to lift that one from both ends simultaneously. Edgar gave Roth a weak smile and puffed air out through pursed lips.

"Edgar, these bags are too long." Leon put the faucet down and held his hands apart. "Two or three feet is enough. Otherwise, they're too heavy."

"That's okay, Mi'ta Rot'. We strong." Gaetana slapped himself on the biceps as he said "strong." He grinned at his sons who kept their grip on the hand truck.

"Yes, but the bags aren't." Roth looked around. "You'll have to tear open these casings and shovel them into large garbage bags. You'd better double the bags up." Gaetana looked down at his chest and flicked off a piece of food.

"We out of garbage bags, Mi'ta Rot'."

"You're out? Why didn't you tell me this morning when I went out for supplies? I would have picked them up."

Edgar shrugged. One more shrug and Roth thought he would lose his mind. "Tell me, Edgar, you think I have nothing better to do than drive back and forth like a yo-yo getting you things? You must think that I work for you, that I'm here to make your life easy, is that it?"

Like his wife's had earlier, Gaetana's face began going stony. He would stand there like a stalagmite.

"You're wasting my time, Edgar. I've got other buildings to get to. Tell me, where have you been all morning? How come no one can ever find you in the morning anymore? What exactly are you doing when you're supposed to be here? If you don't want this job, just say the word. We'll get someone else. No one's forcing you to stay here."

Roth stopped speaking. A blank, inert look had come fully into Gaetana's face. Not only peasants wore that expression; Roth knew it, too. He had worn it himself in the face of his grandfather's interrogations. Those would begin with a small infraction—as minute as a grit of sand plinking into a puddle—like bouncing his ball off the garage door. But the ripples would widen, and his grandfather's face would draw closer and get redder until Leon could feel the hot rancid breath spitting on him. "Can't you see you're making marks on the paint, doing that? Have you ever once thought of washing them off? Your grandmother's a sick woman who loves you. She's trying to sleep. Don't you ever think about her? Don't you ever think of anyone but yourself? Are you the only one who counts around here? How have you turned out to be such a selfish, inconsiderate little boy? Me, me, me all the time! Does anything I say ever get through to you? Answer me! Does it?"

Gaetana stood there, battened down. He poked a piece of garbage with his toe, a coffee filter. Roth looked at the heaps of oozing trash. One of the boys had picked up a snow shovel and was scooping the trash back frantically into the broken bag. Each shovelful slid back to the floor.

"All right, Edgar. All right. Look, until we get some new bags, why don't you just tie off one end of some fresh compactor casing, not too long. After you get it filled, you can tie the open end closed like you do the compacted stuff."

Gaetana went over to the machine and came back with an empty cardboard roll, shaking his head, shocked. He held it out as though he had discovered the offending party in this entire unhappy matter: what are you going to do, he seemed to say, with rolls of plastic that run out this way?

Roth turned up his collar as he went back outside. Snow went down his neck anyway, heavy and wet. It seeped in quickly through the seams of his shoes and soaked his socks. All winter he had meant to waterproof them. He hugged the wall for protection, though it offered none. Halfway to the street, his ankle gave way. He stumbled against the brick. The faucet

102

jabbed into his ribs, pushing the breath out of him. Roth kicked at the snow and unearthed a wadded-up ball, dark at the center.

The other day Gaetana's wife had motioned for Edgar to tell Roth something. Gaetana's fist had begun grinding into the socket of his other palm.

"What is it, Edgar?" he had said.

"My wife say, uh, people throwing things down. Throw things into the courtyard."

"Well, tell them to stop."

Edgar squirmed. His face looked as though ants were crawling over it.

"Well, what are they throwing? Food? Garbage? Should we post a sign in the lobby?"

"No! No garbage. Different things. You know, um, private things." He appealed to his wife who nodded vigorously with satisfaction.

"Like what kind of things? Letters? Mail?"

Edgar shook his head.

It was like playing twenty questions.

"More personal? Clothes? Underpants?"

Edgar began nodding his head violently.

"Underpants? Panties?"

Edgar, agitated, beckoned him to follow. He led Roth out through a side door into the courtyard. Strewn about on the concrete were objects that resembled small nocturnal animals crushed beneath the wheels of cars. An extended family of them. Roth realized he'd never seen sanitary napkins before, used or otherwise. He looked up; all the windows were shut. "Who, Edgar?"

"Estevez, 3, um, 3A, mother *and* daughter."

"Have you said something to them?"

"They don't care."

"How long has this been going on?"

Edgar shrugged.

At first Leon had thought the gesture meant *I don't know.* Now, he knew it meant that he would never be told, that he would never get to the bottom of it. It meant he couldn't ask

Edgar to pick the bloody things up. Maybe Edgar would just do it. After all, he was the super. Leon made a note.

They had gone back into the apartment. Gaetana's wife, the telephone receiver wedged between shoulder and ear, fixed Leon with a stare, glittering with indignation. Leon shook his head and tsked his tongue. He rolled his eyes for good measure. She shook her head, too.

"Animales!" she had hissed.

Standing on his good foot, Roth poked the Kotex with his toe. One of Gaetana's sons, the big one—where did he get his height from?—stood behind him, indifferent, waiting. Impassive as a golem. Roth limped to his car and found two boxes of four-mil garbage bags in the trunk; he sent the boy back with them. His ribs ached as he pulled down on the hatch.

Roth hobbled up the stairs to the third floor. He shifted the faucet to his left arm and rapped loudly on the door of 3A. His toes throbbed with cold. Menses. It sounded like a word he'd never heard before, something biblical, talismanic. He moved his weight off his bad ankle. He pounded on the door.

"Landlord!" he said loudly. "I want to talk to you. Open up."

The woman with the pearl earrings stood in the doorway. She pulled her pink sweater across the bulge of her belly and smiled at Roth. She had such small lips.

"Oh, hello. I thought you might have been the landlord. Sorry to make you wait. I had to lie down, the baby was really moving. He must've been doing back flips or something."

Snow melting in Roth's hair ran down into his eyes. He blinked and stared at her olive cheeks, smooth as the skin on the inside of the thigh; she had the hint of a moustache, a dark fuzz. Her defenselessness filled Roth with violent feeling. What was Gaetana up to?

"The super said you wanted to see me. He said just a mother and daughter lived here. He must have made a mistake."

"No, that's right. I do live here with my mother. Johnny, he's in the Marines. He's stationed down at Fort Bragg. He was just on leave. But he had to go back early this morning. Already I miss him." She crossed her arms tighter and squeezed her shoulders.

"I'm sure you must," Roth mumbled. "Was there something you wanted to see me about?"

"You know, there is something Johnny said I should call the landlord about. The guy upstairs, he plays his radio at five o'clock in the morning, real loud, to help him wake up, you know. Johnny went up there last time he was back and told the guy to turn it down. But he still does it. I have a hard time sleeping anyway, even without the racket he makes."

She rubbed the hard sides of her belly. Leon could sense the tautness of it. It was like a fortress. Amazing that something alive was in there, walled off. Something with a dark, watery life, in a world of its own. This woman was like a living poultice. The sanitary napkins couldn't be coming from here. His ankle hurt.

"The super should talk to him. I can't make him turn it down."

"I told the super. But this guy is a friend of the super's. So, it didn't do no good. He and Johnny ended up shouting at each other. Then for a couple of days, it got louder."

Roth said he'd talk to the super and went down to 2F. The door was shut. He knocked. "Elvin, you there?" No one answered. Roth walked to the stairs, then turned back and knocked again. He put his ear to the door. He couldn't make out a sound. Elvin always sang Gospel. That's why Elvin was so steady. He carried it around with him, his own weather of strong feelings, like being inside a bubble. Leon often walked around an apartment Elvin was painting, pretending to inspect it, really just listening. He kicked the door with his good foot. He kicked it again.

"Elvin!" The name echoed up and down the hall as though he had fallen down a well. He limped upstairs. At 4G no one came to the door. The TV was still going. Roth thought he heard a toilet being flushed. Was the boy there alone? What if he needed a drink? What if he felt too weak to get up? Leon knew what would happen. The boy would call out from bed; that's what children did. He would wait, confident of the familiar sound of his mother's steps. He'd call again, wait, then call louder and, when still no one came, he'd call out even louder, though not yet his loudest. Or maybe the boy had just woken up and forgotten that his mother had gone out. Now it would be dawning on him that he was all alone. Soon he would begin to shout in earnest. He would fill the apartment with his own voice, not waiting between shouts. Soon after that, he would begin shouting at the top of his lungs, the rhythm of his shoutings a kind of comfort, filling the empty space. But he couldn't keep it up all day. Eventually, he would have to stop. The silence, then, would ring in his ears. He'd feel the stillness of his room, its dankness. No one was home. No one was coming home. It wouldn't be long before he was certain that no one would ever be back. Leon felt like calling to the boy, letting him know that someone was there, that someone knew he was there. But maybe calling out to him would alarm the boy even more, would make him think something had happened to his mother, something bad, irreversible.

He fled downstairs, favoring his bad ankle.

eon Roth knocked at 3F. He would check the leak Elvin noticed in the ceiling of 2F. Water was tricky. Sometimes water could run along a riser or a stud and bypass a floor or two altogether. He might have to check the entire line. If the source of the leak remained concealed, you sometimes had to tear up the wall in more than one apartment to find it. He recalled that kitchens and bathrooms were back to back in the F line. As Leon knocked again, he heard the lock turning.

"Landlord!" he called.

The door opened. "Landlord? I thought you said you were the agent for this building?" said Melisandra Velarde.

"Landlord, agent, what's the difference? I came to check for a leak into the apartment below."

"So, a rose by any other name smells just as sweet? Well, Mr. Agent, not to me. When I hear things called by false names, I start feeling for my purse. I don't like false pretenses." She looked him over like a piece of reconditioned merchandise she was considering.

"You're a wet lion, Leon. A wet lion without window guards. Well, come in, why don't you. Dry off."

Roth followed her into the living room. No couch or chairs. No bookshelves or cabinets. Nothing on the walls. It seemed unfurnished.

"Did you just move in here?" asked Leon. Looking down, though, he noticed a railroad tie stretched across the center of the room. A few pillows lay on the floor. And stones. A number of large stones.

"I like to live simply. Just one of each thing. At the most, one. Except for those rocks over there. But, really, there's only one of each of them, too. Now, my daughter's room, that's a whole different story altogether. I'll get you a towel."

The far half of the living room was occupied by large stones, rough ones and smooth ones, some upright, some horizontal, set into some kind of fine gravel. One stood waist-high, a boulder, virtually, glinting with mica. Velarde came back in.

"Here you go, Mr. Sea Lion, catch. Here, give me that," she said, taking the faucet from Roth's hand. "No window guards, but you bring me an old faucet I don't need. Very nice."

"Is that really a rock garden?" asked Roth handing back the towel. He took the faucet from her in return. It was abraded now along the entire length of the spout. Plating flaked off in his hand as he ran his thumb up and down. What was the point of putting it back now? So much for it lasting a lifetime.

"You know about rock gardens?"

"I've read about them, seen pictures."

"My mother thinks I'm crazy. 'You got almost nothing in your apartment except rocks. What do you need rocks for?' she says. 'You got enough rocks in your head. If you like sand, Melisandra, go to the beach.' How about you? Do you think I'm crazy?"

Roth studied the stones. How did she get the big ones up here, he wondered. It would take a dump truck to cart it all away. What a headache that would be. He hoped she wasn't moving out anytime soon.

"Well, it doesn't hurt to be a little bit crazy," he replied.

"You know what I like about it? It leaves you alone. I come home, my daughter's still with my mother for a while yet. I can still hear the grinders going, the nauseating compound they pour in the molds is still in my nose—I work in a dental lab. When I get back here, my hips and shoulders ache from leaning over and sitting on a stool that's too high. Someone talks to me, I just want to bite their head off. Then I look at my little stone zoo, and I know that those rocks couldn't care less that I'm back. They don't give off an ounce of false warmth. You go up to the tigers' cage at the zoo, and one of those big cats looks at you, it's the same thing. You don't matter. But you don't not matter either, you know? I stop feeling sorry for myself. The aches and the smell go away. I mean, they're just rocks, right? But they seem to be putting their attention on something important. I pick a rock and I look at it for as long as I can and try to put my attention on something important, too. You know what I'm talking about, Leon? Or do you think everything's okay just the way it is?"

Leon's rib ached. A rock garden in an apartment in the Bronx.

"Do you know what I'm talking about, Leon?"

"There's a park I go to sometimes, when I knock off work," he replied. "I sit on this one particular bench and look at this one particular tree, I don't even know what kind it is, it doesn't have any leaves. I just kind of let my eyes cross and feel its branches move in the wind, the way it's balanced, they way it holds itself upright. I watch it until I feel like I'm made of wood, too. Whatever's eating at me eats a little less. At least I stop thinking about whether I should say I'm the agent for the building or the landlord." Roth glanced at Velarde and then trained his eyes on the arrangement and spacing of the stones. "It's pretty nice, Melisandra, I like it."

She watched him looking at it. "But what, Mr. Art Critic? Something's bothering you about it."

"I don't know. It could be a little starker, maybe. Less cluttered. That white one by the window could go. Too pretty, if you know what I mean."

"I should tell my mother this. Mom, the agent for the building thinks my apartment's too cluttered. So what's the matter, you don't like things to be beautiful?"

"I like it most where it looks like nature made it, as if the gardener were doing it the way nature would have wanted."

"And what do you know about what nature wants?"

Leon looked down at the swirling furrows she had made in the gravel, probably with her fingers. How did she get all that gravel up here? Rocks were less troublesome than chickens. Ramirez in 5F kept chickens, Gaetana had said. She sold them in the building, eggs, too. Her niece had moved out, and she needed the income. He didn't bother to tell Fein. At least rocks weren't unsanitary. Leon looked up at Melisandra. He noticed a small scar beside each eye, the shape and color of a fingernail paring.

"I don't think nature wants anything," said Leon. "It's only people who do. People want. They want money, a new stove, the upper hand, the good life; they want to live, they want to eat, they want to die, you name it, they want it."

"And what do you want, Mr. Philosopher? And don't tell me you just like to fix faucets."

Leon looked down at the chips of plating stuck to his palm. He tilted his hand from side to side to make them glitter.

"I don't want much," he said, glancing at the stitching of her sweater. "Live in a rock garden, maybe. Heal the sick. Ask how you got those scars next to your eyes. Not much, really. Oh, and find the leak that's running into the apartment below."

"Not a bad list."

"I'm glad you approve."

Roth sat on the edge of the bathtub and ran his finger along the caulking where the tiles met the tub. He checked the grouting between the tiles on the wall.

"So, tell me, Miss Prosecuting Attorney," Leon said, "what do you want? Or do you get to ask all the questions?"

"Find anything?" Melisandra was standing behind him with one foot on the toilet seat.

"No, looks okay to me." Roth unbuttoned his coat. He got on his knees and followed the tile floor along the wall under the sink. He looked up at her. Melisandra sat down on the toilet and put her chin in her hand.

"You know, I like you, Leon. Not many people I know know what a rock garden is. At the dental lab where I work, they're all like my mother. They think I'm nuts."

Leon moved toothbrushes and a Lady Schick razor out of the way and examined beneath the medicine cabinet where the sink joined the wall. "Are you going to answer my question?"

"That's what I'm doing. I don't really want to heal the sick, Leon. Christ or a doctor, I'm not. And this leak doesn't interest me too much. I wouldn't mind some more money, my daughter could use a new winter coat. But that's different from what I'm talking about. What I want, for instance, is that when I tell someone what I want he doesn't suddenly look at me like I was speaking a foreign language. Or else smile and shake his head and tell me what a crazy girl I am or hug me to squelch the talk. Then there are the guys who don't know there's something they're supposed to understand, and the ones who take the cake don't even know there's something they're supposed to *try* to understand."

She got to her feet as if she'd been pricked by a needle. Leon pretended he was still checking the tiles. It always pleased him the way hexagons fit together. He ran his eye over them as if to discover some angles where somehow they didn't mesh, gratified that the laws of geometry held in every case.

"You know what I'm talking about? Did you ever have someone you could really talk to, Leon?"

Leon looked up at her from the floor. He felt like a cockroach too far from its crack. "Yes. I did, once."

"Yeah? Like what sort of stuff did you talk about?"

"Mostly, she talked," said Leon as he wiped at the tiles. "She'd say things like, 'Those who talk don't know. Those who know don't talk.'"

"What's that supposed to mean?"

"Or here's another thing she said: 'Thinking's overrated. Mostly it's been used to make us like machines.'"

"She said that?"

Leon shrugged. "One time we drove to this park for the day, up by Bear Mountain. We didn't talk exactly. It was more like a meeting of minds. We scrambled up a steep boulder on the side of a hill and hunkered down there, pretending we were birds of prey. We sort of pecked and cooed at each other, and when it drizzled we threw a blanket over our shoulders to make a kind of nest. Sometimes we swooped down on unsuspecting prey, mostly dogs. I don't think we used any words at all. It was a whole day of bird talk."

"I ask you if you ever really talked with someone, and you recite to me some high falutin' gibberish and tell me about bird talk."

"So, that sounds strange to you?"

"Not so strange. But it is pretty strange as an example of conversation."

"I've been trying to figure out if it was really special or not, that sort of thing."

"You were birds, huh? Killer birds. And did you do it like killer birds, up there on that rock? Did you know that eagles do it falling out of the sky?"

"No. It was just a two-of-us-against-the-world kind of thing."

"Sounds pretty innocent to me. Kind of sweet. Everybody has games like that. Some seem more interesting than others. So, is this girl dead or something?"

Leon traced hexagons with his finger, each one identical, endless, like a repeating decimal. "Or something."

"And now you want to live in a rock garden and heal the sick."

"I wouldn't mind."

"Well, she must have really done a number on you if you can't figure out what happened." Melisandra began pacing in the tight confine between Leon and the toilet, tapping a hand rapidly against her thigh.

"Well, Mr. Nature Lover, you want to know how I came by those scars on the side of my eyes? I'm going to tell you."

Leon staggered up to his feet. "Okay, but tell me in the kitchen. I need to look under the sink. I can't find any kind of leak in here."

Roth opened the cabinet doors under the double sink. Sponges, a Brillo box, floor wax, shoe polish tins, Mr. Clean. He moved them out of his way and slid under on his back and shined a flashlight up at the hot and cold water connectors. Melisandra's feet bumped against his legs, and he heard the hollow drumming of water filling a pot. The back of his head felt wet.

"Leon," she said, putting water on the stove, "you don't know nothing about killer birds. They're big and graceful, they got broad, beautiful wings, and they're not bothered by anything because they are strong, and they know it. They got talons, a beak that can tear anything apart. But because they're beautiful, you forget they're killers. Dream all you like, Leon. You're just a sparrow. A sparrow playing at being a hawk. So, what will it be, tea or instant coffee?"

Water ran in the sink above him. It sounded like Melisandra was scouring out mugs. Drops came down on Leon's neck from around the sink strainer. "Coffee'll do," he said.

"Let me tell you about killers. I met this guy at a Puerto Rico independence rally. I still believe in that, not the bombing stuff but the principle of the thing. He was standing next to me in the crowd. We went out afterwards. This guy could really talk. He talked about dignity and rights and freedom. Lots of calm righteousness. Lots of graceful anger. He really wowed me. I never believed in any of that Oh-baby!-you-so-beautiful! love shit. Here was a guy I could tell was going to do something important. And he could be funny, too, you know? He'd meet me after school. He'd do me to the tune of this great future we were going to be a part of making. I'd wait around for him to call, to come by—pretty soon I'd stopped going to school so we could be together. I'd do anything for that guy. I did a lot of waiting. He kept me on a string. He worked down at the flower mart, and he'd bring me beautiful bouquets of flowers. My mother worked weekends. One day we're making it he says, let's pretend you're a cop who's trying to bust me, or better, he says, turning me over, pretend you're the mayor, pretend you're Ed Koch. That seemed funny to me, so I imitate Koch, you know the way he talks, How'm I doing and all that. Well, he shoves my face into the pillow, and he drives into me from behind. He calls me a pig while he's doing it. What'ya think of this, Mr. Mayor, how'm I doing? he asks over and over. He tore me up. I was sore for days. You listening, Leon? Or is this too much for a killer bird like you?"

Water from the cold water supply was dripping onto his cheek. Leon lay there, letting it run down onto his collar. He would have to get a basin wrench to reach the compression fitting. "Yes. I can hear you. I think I've found the trouble. I may need some putty to really fix it." He tried to get his offset on the sink strainer nut to tighten it.

"Very good, Mr. Managing Agent. I'm going to give you one of my daughter's gold stars."

Leon could hear Melisandra moving about the kitchen.

"What do you think, Leon. Did I stop seeing this guy after that? Did I? I was crazy about him. Afterwards, I think I was even crazier about him. Isn't that really crazy? The weirdness attracted me. I didn't think it had anything to do with me. And he always acted like nothing had happened. You know when I finally realized he was bad news? We're doing it one day, and he says, you be Richard Nixon, and I say, let's not, let's not today, and he says okay, tell you what, I'll be Nixon. He begs me to let him have it, so I get on top and start ranking on him, calling him a pig, shaking his jowls, playing, you know, relieved it wasn't going to happen again. Suddenly, he throws me down and starts squeezing my head between his hands saying, just like he's Nixon, I am not a crook, and I think maybe he's just kidding but then he says that he's had enough of my people, that we've had it too good, that's the problem, that we're a lazy people who don't know the value of work, we just want to lie around in the sun and get high and fuck and he's going to teach us a lesson and he begins hammering my forehead with his like it's a coconut or something. I try to twist away but he squeezes my head harder between his hands and he pounds my face like he's driving nails and soon there's blood on his face, and he's yelling you fucking spic, you fucking spic cunt, you'll do what I say and like it, this is America, this is America, this is America, and then there's blood in my eyes and I can't see a thing. I don't remember anything after that. But I can still feel where his thumbnails went in," she said, touching each temple lightly with her fingertips.

Leon squirmed out from under the sink and leaned back against the cabinet door. His face was wet, and the back of his shirt was drenched inside his jacket. She was squatted down in front of him. The tea kettle was spluttering with steam.

"What do you think of that, Leon the sparrow? You like that kind of love talk? You'd never do a thing like that, would you? Would you? You don't got some closet where you keep all the body parts hidden, do you? Don't go silent on me. What's the matter? The cat got your tongue?"

She rocked forward onto her knees. She seized Leon's head by the temples. Her face was close to his. She was breathing hard through her nostrils.

"You don't fool me," said Leon. His voice came out clogged with phlegm. "You don't fool me at all, Melisandra. You're a sparrow, too."

Leon could smell a vapor of soap and sweat and heat rising from inside her sweater. Her fingers felt icy on his ears. The scars had whitened beside her eyes as she looked at him; they were so symmetrical they might have been forceps marks. Melisandra's face came toward him and Leon shut his eyes. She put her forehead to his and pressed with all her might.

Hello? Fein Realty."

"Ellen, it's Leon."

"Leon! It's about time! Where have you been? Mr. Fein is just about out of his mind. When are you coming in?"

"I've been busy, Ellen. Anyway, it's only one o'clock. What's the big deal? Did you give Miguel my message?"

116

"It's a bigger deal than you think. Mr. Fein wants to talk with you. Mr. Fein! It's Leon. Okay. Hang on, Leon. I'm going to transfer you."

Roth sandwiched the receiver between his ear and shoulder and stretched his hands out on the workbench. The wall that had once hung with tools was bare except for a plastic Jesus. It was meant to look emaciated but the glossiness of the plastic made the figure seem well-fed, satisfied. Its too-big head, festive and grotesque, flopped to the side, as if it, too, had been holding a receiver, one that someone had taken away. Roth heard clicking on the line, then Ellen's voice call his name, then Fein's booming voice, then the line went dead or he was on hold again.

Roth tapped his fingertips together, waiting. The bristliness of Melisandra's cropped hair still tingled on the palms of his hands. His head had felt as though it was splitting open like an unripe cantaloupe. It had taken all his strength to force her head back. A fierce, exultant expression had transformed her face. It was like watching a dog become a fox. She pushed forward again until their lips met. Still, she pushed. Leon felt that if he let go her mouth would mangle itself against his. Leon resisted with his mouth, tightening his lips, but Melisandra ground her face against his. Panicky, he yanked her sideways. He was on top of her then, half under the sink. A drop of cold water splattered on the back of his neck. On the stove the kettle was choking on steam. A hard pelvic bone thrust against his.

"Leon the pussy-cat," she said, tracing with her fingers the cartilage of his ears. "You better be careful. This isn't no mouse you're playing with."

"Hello, hello? Leon? Allan? Pick up on 9878, Allan, no, on 9878." The line went dead again. Roth rubbed his hands together. Melisandra's head had felt the same to his hands as Magda's had when she had cut her hair off.

"Do you know what hair is, Leon?" Magda had said, as she snicked at the last few clumps. Blood crusted in small rosettes where she had gouged her scalp with the nail clippers. Hair lay in a heap on the floor. She scooped some of it up and held it out to Leon as if it were the feathers of a bird.

"Hair is the mind's thoughts, Leon. Everything that happens—thoughts, feelings, the whole works—it's all braided together and told in the language of proteins. You're in here too, Leon. And every day that I've been in this hell hole has also been preserved." Magda put her ear to the dark fluff in her hands.

"Do you know that you can hear protein? The scalp is like a tape recorder, Leon, and hair is the tape; it keeps on playing what's been recorded on it, over and over.

"Listen! Even cut off it doesn't stop. It's like the circles of hell. I hate it. I don't want to hear it anymore." Magda stuffed the hair into the wastebasket. She brushed off her robe, got on her knees and swept up all the clippings with her hands. Leon watched her meticulously pick up every last hair.

Magda's mother had committed her after Leon had been to the house. It was a year before he was able to see her. She appeared in the meeting area, escorted by an attendant. She was pale and heavy, her dense hair pulled severely into a bun. They sat in over-stuffed, dusty armchairs. Leon concentrated on the rain falling on the steps, on the lawn that ran unbroken to a high, stone wall. It was hard to conjure up the Magda he had known, the defiant one who had pulled him to her breast, the one who wore her Mets cap backwards to play ball with her younger brother, and who on a dare had taken the train in from Brooklyn after midnight to walk the lip of the 59th Street fountain with him. This Magda, the Magda who had seared her own flesh, and the rocking Magda, were crowding her out.

"Leon," Magda said at last, "what have you been doing with yourself? You look almost as bad as I do."

He shrugged and gave her a deprecating smile. They walked the halls, Magda guiding him through the uniform corridors. It was a large institution, and Leon had no idea where they were. Then she put a finger to her lips and led him into a room and shut the door. "It's not much, but it's home," she said. It was surprising how unoccupied her room appeared, nothing on the walls, no propped photographs or jewelry case on the bureau.

"That's what a place like this is all about, Leon. It makes a constant statement that you don't count and that you'd better get used to it. So," she turned to face him with that bright, conspiring look he recalled so well, "a little subversion never hurts." She tugged him by the belt over to the bed. Once he was inside her, however, she lay there with her eyes closed, stiffly unmoving. Angrily, he made himself not stop.

Afterwards she told him she wasn't allowed anything sharp, they watch you like a hawk. She asked him for his nail clippers. Even though the voices had stopped, they still treated her like some kind of unpredictable circus animal. She jumped through all their hoops, but they still kept their whips at the ready. "I'm not crazy," she said. "I see how they look at me. They don't believe I'm better. They think I'm just trying to fool them. Leon, I've got to get out of here. I just have to."

Leon came to see her regularly after that. Mostly they walked the grounds. The last time he saw her, however, Magda was wearing a tasseled kerchief on her head when she came out to meet him.

"Don't I look like a Polish peasant ready to pull potatoes?" she asked, twirling in a drab, pleated skirt. "Honestly, I wouldn't mind. I'm just not stupid or Catholic or down-to-earth enough." In her room, she turned and stood before him undoing the knot beneath her chin slowly, smiling. A thrill went through Leon. It was like the old Magda had suddenly reappeared. But when the kerchief fell away, almost all of Magda's long, black hair was gone. She looked to Leon like the French women after the liberation he'd seen pictures of, who had slept with Nazis and had their heads shaved for it. He had held her head in his hands, as if her hair would reappear if he touched it. She looked at him triumphantly and began snipping by feel an uncut part behind her ear. Leon felt mutilated. He had thought, somehow, that he had been helping her. But in the drama she was living, he had only a walk-on part. Maybe he was only there to change the set between scenes, to provide props.

"Leon? Leon!" Fein's voice elbowed through the phone,

"Where in God's name have you been? The one day I have urgent need to be in touch with you and you don't check in."

"I've been busy, Allan. Very busy."

"Where? Where has this busyness nailed you to the wall, Leon?"

Roth glanced up at the miniature God hanging patiently on the pegboard. "162nd Street."

"All day, so far? You're telling me you've been at 162nd Street all day?"

"All morning. All morning, so far. It's only one o'clock."

"One twenty-three. What do you think, you're the super, Leon? You want to be a super? I can arrange that. Just tell me. And of all the places to spend the day, you pick 162nd Street. Of all the places!"

"The building needs the attention, Allan. If we had a decent super running it, I wouldn't have to be here. No one spent time here when Schmidt was super." Roth looked to see that the door was closed. It wouldn't do for Gaetana to hear this. All he needed was a morale problem on top of everything else.

"It doesn't matter anymore. I want you to stop with whatever repairs you're doing. All orders for materials, I want you to cancel them. Get in touch with Elvin and tell him to send his nephew to Jerome Avenue instead, tomorrow morning. Anyway, the people who wanted 2F backed out."

"What's up?"

"Leon, we're selling the building. In fact, we're closing on it this evening. I was going to tell you earlier, but the whole deal came together very suddenly."

"You're selling it? What the hell for, Allan? It's a good building."

"For one thing, it's taking too much of your time, Leon. It's eating us alive."

"It's not an insoluble problem, Allan. It's very specific."

"We're stuck with him. You know that Gaetana is Diaz's wife's brother-in-law. I can't offend Diaz. The Spanish are very touchy when it comes to their honor. Plus the union would give us grief on it. It cost us a bundle to get rid of Mulligan over at Burnside Avenue. That guy was really killing us."

"Who are we selling it to, Allan?"

"Joseph Hakim and some associates of his."

"Hakim? You mean the guy who owns the building that backs onto ours on 173rd?"

"Yeah."

"You've got to be kidding? He'll wreck this place. Allan, you didn't go into that one. Hakim is sucking it dry. Squatters and junkies are camping out in gutted apartments. He's even hitting them up for rent. He'll do the same thing here."

"That building was on its way down when he bought it, Leon. It would have taken too much to fix it."

"And you think he'll take care of this one?"

"That's his business, Leon. He owns it now."

"He's a creep, Allan. He doesn't give a rat's ass."

"He's in business like the rest of us, Leon. Grow up. I want you out of there. Any tools of ours, put them in your car. Be quiet about it. And don't tell Gaetana. Finish up and get going. The closing's going to take place here at six. Oh, and I want you to forget about the Obergon eviction. Hakim has agreed to take care of it. Let Obergon be his headache."

oth stood on the threshold of 2F and smelled its vacancy. Dust and camphor and that most obliterating of smells, freshly applied paint—Elvin must have begun on the primer. His footsteps rang as he walked across the floor. Flakes of yellowed off-white speckled the floors. An empty apartment always made Roth feel stricken. A person could live here thirty years and yet disappear without a trace. Some Lysol and a coat of semi-gloss is all it would take. The rooms throbbed with emptiness. He'd read somewhere that amputated limbs were supposed to do that, throb as though they were still there, very specific pains in the calf or shin where there wasn't a calf or shin to hurt anymore. If you put your hand where someone's leg had been, you would feel your hand and they would feel their leg: two different bodies occupying the same spot. Leon thought about that a lot.

His grandfather had died while Leon was on the way to the hospital. When he got there the sheets were already stripped from the bed. At first Leon thought he'd been moved to a new room. The old guy had lain there the night before staring in terror at something in the air between them, mouthing the word, *ma-ma*, over and over. Sour-breathed. Over sixty years since he'd seen her and he was again calling, *ma-ma*. Could anything be worse? All the intervening years may as well not have happened.

Leon couldn't remember his own mother. He had a single picture of her, and it had long ago taken the place of his memories, if he ever had any. She was dressed in an austere brown suit, looking away from the camera and smoking a cigarette as if everything that mattered to her was outside the frame of the snapshot. Her dark hair was pulled back tightly behind her head and heightened a serious, probing look Leon associated with people who gaze out at the ocean. All that Leon had in common with her was this feeling that everything important was happening beyond his sight, outside the frame. But it also made him feel sick. He, too, had belonged to the realm of the unimportant, to things that were in her way. She was looking beyond him. Yet he felt that if he possessed the same degree of yearning the photo hinted at, he, too, in her position, would have looked beyond a child like himself. Instead, he had grown up to take care of his grandparents; he took care of buildings; he had stayed by Magda. It was just as well—he would probably have taken care of his mother, too. If she'd known this about him then, she might have taken him with her. "Leon, be a dear and get me a …" he could somehow hear her say to him without taking her eyes off the restless waves.

Leon sat on the radiator cover in the larger bedroom and watched the snow. It was still coming down without let-up. It looked as though it were being poured from a bucket, but it swirled and looped upward as much as it fell, riotous, a roller-coaster. Leon's head spun, maybe from the paint. Wind sucked and shoved at the pane of glass, rattling the sash in its track. Swoop all they liked, those flakes of snow would come to rest somewhere. Roller coasters ran on tracks. He'd be the guy who walked the tracks every morning before the Cyclone opened to make sure the bolts were snug, the wooden ties secure. Others would scream in the curves, their pink, wet mouths opened wide. He'd be the one to worry about the vibration and the cumulative effect of G-force on the scaffolding. Let someone else put up with Gaetana. It was-n't his to worry about anymore. Maybe it wouldn't be so bad. It would take a while to run a good building into the ground. The tenants would see the writing on the wall and some would leave, hard as that was to do. The girl in 3A and her army Johnny would get a place of their own, take the mother with them. Bonforty would go, too. Had she come home yet? He'd check before he left. He could feel the boy breathing through his egg-white eyes.

The snow, as Roth followed particular flakes of it, seemed buoyant, mercurial, free of wear. So what that it settled, melted, ran, eventually, into the Bronx River, then out the Spuyten Duyvil? What didn't end up out at sea, that great, absorbing emptiness skimmed over by hungry gulls? Some people ended up with nothing. You lift up a shell and nothing is under it. You lift another. Each time you lift one up, nothing's there. But even if you picked up the right shell and did win, what could you win that would match the wish to win? Money? Magda's smile? The life of falling snow? Wishing was like a Ferris wheel; it went round and round. Leon felt like he'd come to the end of the line. That's what made the snow so gay. It was taking a thrilling ride, and then it was going to come to rest. Pure cessation. If it was part of a cycle, it was a long, slow cycle.

The radiator he was sitting on was cold; it pulled at his hams—the big boiler, dormant three floors below, was in its afternoon off-cycle. Leon leaned back against the window frame and cupped his tender knee in his hands.

He heard the door to the apartment open and footsteps cross the threshold and stop. He kept quiet, hoping it was Elvin and that he would start humming, but Elvin would have walked right in. It was remarkable how the tenants kept an eye on things. People lived behind closed doors, but the least thing out of the ordinary, like this door left ajar, and someone was sure to check on it. Roth heard the door shut and movement in the kitchen—cabinets pulled open, taps turned on and off; by the sound of it, someone was looking in the hall closet, then the living room. Someone was walking slowly along the walls, stepping them off, a woman's foot, maybe comparing the size of these rooms to her own. Any other time Roth would have hurried to intercept them, thrust out a stiff *Can I help you?* and got them out of there.

Let them look, he thought. It's over. Maybe he would pack his car and drive out of the city, have a look around: upstate, the Berkshires; Southern Ohio, he'd heard, was pretty, hilly. Trillium bloomed there, he remembered reading somewhere. He didn't know what trillium looked like, but he liked the sound of it. He had skills, some money saved. You could be on your own anywhere.

Whoever it was went into the bathroom; the medicine chest swung open on a squeaky hinge. He heard the explosive rush through the flushometer, tested, he hoped, not used. That would add to the embarrassment when it was discovered the apartment was not empty. Leon closed his eyes. Let them find him here, a small shock. He would pretend that he was the one who was surprised. That always worked best. These vacant rooms, though, amplified everything—sound, silence, feeling. Well, awkwardness had come to seem normal, the medium of all relations. Even something as simple as buying the morning paper, Leon had to clear his throat, force the words out as though he hadn't spoken in years. He'd never gotten used to encounters like this one about to take place, but you did it enough times and a scab formed. He glanced out at the acrobatic snow and shut his eyes again. They'd get through it. A little talk, an awkward smile, a spell of awkward silence. Then he'd shut the door. There would be no future meetings to remind them. He wouldn't be coming back again.

Roth felt her halt in the doorway to the bedroom. He waited for some small exclamation, some sign he had been seen, before he turned his head and apologized for scaring her; he'd explain how he came to be sitting there, say something about all the snow, until the discomfort was gone. He would lock the door as they went out, put the key back in the workroom. If Gaetana or one of his kids wasn't shoveling the walk, it was no skin off his back. He would make no more notes, throw that notebook away. Most of the notes he made came from this building anyway. He was out of here. He waited for his cue to set things right.

No sound came from the doorway. Roth listened for the gritty scrape of shoe on wood, rustle of clothes, cough, something. Nothing broke the quiet. He imagined he could hear soft puffs of breathing. He remained in his pose, cradling his knee with clasped hands, and hoped he looked lost in thought. Roth often feigned unawareness when he felt he was being looked at. When at last he turned his head, he would find himself alone, unobserved, the presence something he had imagined. He listened hard. Maybe she was gone. Or hadn't yet come into the room. He'd better get to his feet before whoever this was did appear. His back was getting twinges and his wrists felt numb. He swung around, relieved to move, and saw her leaning against the door jamb staring at him, those same eyes from this morning. Morales's daughter.

"I saw the door open," she said. "I was curious what it was like in here."

Roth watched her cross in front of him with casual ease, hands in her pockets, and lean her head inside the closet. The black seams of her fishnet stockings ran up the center of her muscled calves and widening thighs and disappeared under the skirt. She stood there, her back to Roth, as if to let him look.

"Hey, this is roomy. The room I share with my sister isn't much bigger than this closet. This apartment really rented?" Ringlets of orange-red hair had come loose and hung down damply behind her ear like springs stretched out of shape. She drew her face out of the closet doorway and turned her eyes on Roth. They were like binoculars, trained on him but unseeing, as if no one were looking through them. It made him uncomfortable to feel scrutinized and dismissed at the same time; it disturbed him—her nonchalance, and his own nervousness. She had a husky voice.

"It was rented. But that fell through. The people don't want it anymore."

"Yeah? It's free? Bobby's got himself a good job. He drives a van, you know, doing deliveries. He could afford a place like this. Easy."

"What are you going to do, marry him?"

Morales's daughter moved over to the window beside Roth and checked out the view. The pasty schmaltz of make-up on her cheeks had rubbed away. The skin was bad, pocked and erupted; it had a grayish tinge. She had on different earrings now, large turquoise-colored half-moons. She nestled her hands deeper in her jacket pockets and lifted her padded shoulders.

"I might."

"And what, drop out of school?"

She craned forward appraising the view. The snow was coming down too heavily to see the street. She glanced at Roth who had sat back down on the edge of the radiator. "I don't go no more. Sitting at a desk all day doesn't interest me. It's old."

"So what does hold your interest?"

She gave Roth a hard, insolent look. The girl traced circles with a fuchsia fingernail on the breath-fogged windowpane.

"Your parents know?"

"They don't know nothing. My father, he'd throw a fit if he found out. But he don't care. All he cares about is his cock fights. The lady upstairs keeps the birds for him. Some of the supers around here let them use their basements. He ain't said more than two words to me in months. I got a part-time job at a luncheonette place over by Evander Childs. My mom suspects, but she don't say nothing. I put some of the money in her purse now and then. It keeps her quiet. But why I do it is 'cause they fight less. You ain't going to tell?"

Roth shrugged. The girl began doodling hearts on the pane. Beads of condensate ran down. Roth moved behind her. Peroxide, perfume, conditioner wafted out from the dampness of her head. He couldn't any longer smell the apartment or the paint. It didn't matter who had lived here. He placed his hands on her waist. So narrow. If he squeezed, he felt his thumbs would meet. He ran his middle fingers over the bones of her hips.

The girl kept drawing, arrows now, some through hearts; all the shapes overlapped, dissolving. "You really the landlord, or what?"

Leon slid his arms across the flatness of her belly. He pulled her back against him, his sight blotted out in the density of her hair. His upper lip and eyelids itched. Wetted down like a cat, she'd be tiny.

"So, are you going to let Bobby rent the apartment?" She had stopped drawing. Roth bunched her flimsy skirt up on her hips and slid his fingertips down along her creases inside the panties he imagined were those red ones that had swung from her ankle. He leaned in on her until his hands met. He had somehow imagined the girl didn't have any hair between her legs; it was hot there like shower water.

She put her hands against the sides of the window to steady herself. "You got to tell me if Bobby can have this place. I can't live another day at home. The way he looks at me. He don't say a word, but I see him leering, drunk and stinky when I'm combing my hair sometimes. I make sure I'm not in the apartment when he's there by himself. And I seen him look at my sister. But she don't get it. She's just glad to be getting some attention, you know. She laughs when he tickles her. She squirms, but he don't stop. He tickles her till she cries. While she's lying there doubled over rubbing where he dug his fingers in hard, he just looks at me and grins. I don't trust him. He was looking through my drawers one day, and when I seen him doing it, he tells me he's just making sure I don't have no birth control pills or nothing hidden there. If I catch you it's all over, you gonna wish you was dead, he says and storms out. But that don't worry me. He don't care a damn, really. It's just a show. What's got me worried is that my period is really late. I don't even feel like it's coming. I can't just stay there, I can't. I can't. You gotta let Bobby have this place so I can get out of there. I got nowhere else to go. Oh, what am I going to do, then? I'm fucked. I'm fucked. I'm fucked."

Roth's hands moved slowly back to her waist while she talked. Sensation left his fingertips and went back into his head. He held her now as she slumped over and her legs let go. He lowered her to the floor. She lay on her side sobbing as Roth kneeled next to her, absently patting her shoulder. Her skirt was still hitched up. He stared at the red panties. The lacy part twisted on her hip. The girl's stomach heaved, trembling. As slim as she was, there was a soft bulge of flesh below the hollow of her belly button; a wispy line of black hairs descended from it.

"You want the apartment?" Roth said, watching her tummy shudder with each gasp. They would have to cut the baby out of a body that small. Magda was bigger. But he still couldn't imagine it. Magda as mother. Himself as father. The joint pillbox of family life. Looking out through its small aperture. If you went through the motions long enough, maybe the feelings would follow. Velarde, all alone, was managing. He had to hand it to her. Roth laid his hand lightly on the girl's skin, the raised pores grazing his palm as it traveled over her curves. The air had grown chilly.

"You really want it?" Roth repeated.

She stopped crying and rolled onto her back. She stared at him, expressionless, with those binocular eyes. It wasn't that they were unseeing, exactly; they were simply sizing him up. He was an open book, doing just what she expected, even up there on the roof. She had him pegged. She lay, waiting. Roth thought of her father. He marveled that Morales hadn't seemed to feel his pants coming down as the kids tugged on them, the crack of his ass visible. The stained, jagged teeth. Roth stood over the languid girl. He sucked at his own teeth and tasted something rotten in his mouth. He bent over and pulled the girl to her feet. There was no surprise or worry on her face at all.

"There's nothing I can do for you," he said.

Alarm came into her face. She caught hold of his shirt and pressed the back of her hand against his chest.

"I'm sorry, Miss. I can't help you." He turned her and pushed her lightly between the shoulder blades toward the door.

"Go on. Get out of here. I can't do anything for you."

She looked back over her shoulder as he ushered her out, not frightened now but frail, abandoned. Her large eyes that couldn't keep anything out. A kid's eyes. The bewildered eyes of something having gone wrong. Like the girl on the gurney. Then her face hardened. The binoculars came back up into place. The large eyes that saw through everything. She nodded her head at him, once more the tough cookie.

"You can't do nothing, is right. You think you're so high and mighty. You think you call all the shots. Well, you could have had anything you wanted. But you don't do nothing for me. You're pathetic. Man, I pity you." Roth watched her pivot smartly on her heels and clatter away, her ass chafing in its tight red skirt. He swung the door fully closed this time.

Roth sat down with his back against the front door; it faced into the kitchen. Morales's daughter had left all the cabinet doors open. Like a calling card. She'd left all the closets open, too, and water running in the sink. Roth smiled at the insolence. Someone was here, motherfucker, it seemed to say. It was a kind of mark. A sad little mark. A defamation.

131

From his shirt pocket he drew out an airmail envelope and extracted a sheet of paper. It was crinkly, onionskin, the lightweight kind used for overseas mail. Roth unfolded the letter with care. Since he received it last month, he had frequently taken it out just to stare at it. Sometimes he read it through; others, he simply gazed at her signature.

When she had hacked off her hair, the institution convinced her parents that she wasn't ready to be released. She had relapsed after that, or cutting her hair that way was itself the sign of her relapse. Leon hadn't seen her since, though once, soon after, he had driven out there after work. At the reception desk they had told him that Miss Serce wasn't permitted to have visitors. Leon sat down in the same desiccated, over-plush chairs where she had first come out to see him. He waited. He tried to imagine living there. Half hospital, half train station. It could make a person go mad.

The trouble with psychology, Leon, is that it thinks everything's in your head. I mean, just look at this place. It's real, all too real. The thing is, it doesn't take long before it gets inside your head.

He had watched the sun go down, slanting behind the high brick wall, and still he sat, sinking lower in his lumpy chair. He was waiting, he knew, for Magda to appear. He imagined her brightening at the sight of him, taking his arm, free to go. He would push open the doors into the breezy air, and together they would walk out into the world of possibility. Over and over he replayed this scene, never getting beyond the parking lot or the gates before it dissolved, unimaginable. Each time he ran it, like a silent film, it was accompanied by the stirring and forceful opening chords of one of Chopin's polonaises, the chords of a patriotism that understood what fortitude and heroism meant in an atmosphere of prolonged historical defeat. The Poles had specialized in this, he'd learned through Magda. For Leon, only desperation could make a useless and glorious gesture worth trying.

And then he realized that his soundtrack was not issuing solely from his head. Above the muted buzz of voices, he could hear, faintly, the strains of a piano playing the same polonaise. Over one particularly difficult chord, the pianist faltered, just as Magda with her small hands had faltered all that summer; it was not so much a faltering, really, as a hesitation to assure that the chord was struck exactly right. Leon had begun to think of that retard as part of the piece, part of the drama of obstacles overcome.

Hearing it now, Leon got to his feet as if commanded. He left the reception area and followed the music down a corridor. It grew louder, and to his mind, more forceful, took on more feeling. If it was Magda, could she sense his coming? Had she, too, been hoping, waiting for this moment, counting on him to arrive? Was this piece of music a signal? He began to walk faster, suppressing an urge to run as the music grew nearer.

Before he reached its source, Leon's way was blocked by two attendants who stood as if they had trained for these moments, shoulder to shoulder. "Excuse me, sir," one of them said with a practiced politeness, "do you have a pass to come into this area? No one is allowed here without a pass. And you must be accompanied by a nurse, a case worker or authorized patient."

He was so close. What would Kosciusko do in this situation? A Pole famous enough to have a bridge in Brooklyn named after him. Leon had driven over it into Green Point a hundred times. Each time Magda made him pronounce it correctly in Polish. He'd pause in the middle to get it right, like Magda did her chord. He'd never gotten it. *Koshchooshko.* A general and a patriot who had helped the Americans in their revolution but was unable to save his own country. No one here ever said his name right.

Leon considered the two attendants—one tall, one wide; they were waiting for him to make a move. In a place like this, everyone is suspect, anyone could blossom into bizarre behavior. Pushing past them wouldn't work. Maybe if he began shouting her name. Would she come running when she heard his voice? Even if she couldn't reach him, he would know that she was trying if the piano player broke off. If she managed against the odds to reach him, or he her, would they rush into each other's arms? Embraced and embracing, what then? Would it take an entire phalanx of attendants to pry them apart? O brave Kosciusko! No, they would still have to reckon with each other, off the stage of history.

"You are going to have to leave, sir. No one is permitted to be here without proper authorization. If there's someone you wish to see, they can help you at the desk." Just then, the piece came to its rousing end and, without pause, began over with the abruptness of a record needle stuck in a groove.

What was the use? Everything stood in their way, themselves included. Suddenly, Leon didn't know what he had hoped to accomplish by coming. He turned to go. He felt Mutt and Jeff following close behind, poised to grab him by the armpits. If they locked him up, Leon was certain that he'd never be let out. There was a fine line between Magda's condition and his own; she just happened to satisfy the social definition of insanity: an inability to deal with the things you can't deal with. It was all Leon could do not to run. But inside or out, what did it matter? His life, he felt, was as on hold as anyone's in that loony bin.

When Magda's letter appeared at work, Leon could scarcely comprehend that two years had gone by since he had seen her, so often was she in his thoughts. He had torn open the letter with a mixture of dread and deliverance. Now he carefully unbent the crinkled pages. Before he read it with Talmudic attention, he raised his eyes and surveyed the vacancy of the apartment.

His own wasn't much different from this one. His was dingier and smaller. He owned a clock radio, a frameless mattress, a table and two chairs, dishes in the sink, stacks of old newspapers, a battered dresser. He had neither furnished nor decorated it beyond bare necessity. It looked no different from the day he had moved in. It looked, instead, as though someone were in the process of moving out.

He smoothed Magda's letter on his knee. "Leon," it began. Even that hurt. Just "Leon."

> For the longest time I thought I would send you just a snapshot, no letter at all, so you could see what my hair looks like now that it has grown back. On principle I am letting it grow though I keep the bangs short. I don't really like to see it even from the corner of my eye. But sending a picture seemed

unfair. The fact is, I was angry and wanted to make you feel bad. Yes, bad. And as angry as I felt. But I realize that's not possible. Feeling was never your strong suit.

I can see you reading this and getting that puzzled look on your face, thinking: *Angry? Me, angry?* You always just imagined you were trying to figure something out, but actually you were looking for some crevasse to toss your rage into.

Oh, you were so patient and so loyal, Leon. But you never really understood what I wanted. You were there, yes. Faithful as a hound. No one could fault you for that. But I wanted you to be more than just a good soldier. I wanted you to throw in your lot with me. I wanted you to be wholehearted, not loyal. I wanted you to want something of me. Maybe you did and I just didn't know it. But I wanted you to be my way out, to hold up the roof as the sky came down around me. That's too much to ask of anyone, I know. You couldn't solve my problems even if you had been a different sort of person. I wanted a clean start, free of my family, free of myself. "Our long national nightmare is over," said the ersatz prez who couldn't talk and chew gum at the same time. I wanted my own personal nightmare to end. Everything seemed so dirty, so corrupt, so ugly. It still does, if you want to know the truth, but I feel differently about it now, not so cornered. You didn't like the world either, Leon, but somehow you could bear it. You were always good at going into suspended animation.

Do you know why I really cut off my hair? This is going to sound crazy (ha-ha), but it's not, really. A head of hair, for me, its thousands of strands parallel, tangled, parted, braided, knotted up, began to seem like history—each of us just one of those strands. I couldn't comb it out. Nothing went the way I wanted it to—school, my family, you, politics, the psycho ward. I couldn't seem to make anything I wanted happen. My fantasy of cutting off my hair was that it would give me a clean slate. I can barely recall that feeling of how urgent it seemed. Well, everything was out of whack with me then. Now my hair has grown back. It always grows back. There's no stopping it. Did you know that even when you die, your hair keeps growing? Yes, the dead lie in their coffins and hair falls into their eyes. I'm learning to live with that. I don't know if you understand what I am trying to tell you. You're a fatalist, Leon. You don't think anything will ever change. Yourself, either.

I ran into Andy the other day here in Chicago, and he told me what you were doing, or not doing. I can't believe that you're still in the Bronx, doing the landlord thing. Leon, don't waste your life even if you don't believe in it. You couldn't save me. No one can save anyone else.

My story is simple. I got out a year ago. I met someone, someone who used to visit his brother, a sad, morose guy named Saul who I befriended; we got engaged in September. I wanted to tell you, but I couldn't. I'm working, and I'm back in school, part-time. I'm not happy, but I'm sane. I'm not in love exactly, but I'm satisfied. You were my love. But all of that isn't any longer part of the world. That's how I manage. There's a certain pleasure, though, in going through the motions with competence. I want to work with kids. For them it's not too late. I need to believe that. Where I was is only one kind of nuthouse. There are others. Don't stay locked up in your own. You are your own keeper. Don't forget that you've got the keys to the kingdom. You should have left me, Leon. All those letters, those lonely letters you sent me, Leon! I had to stop reading them. At first I thought they were about us, the way you recalled the things we did. But soon it became clear they were only about you, wishful versions of a reality that wasn't worth banking on. And yet, they kept me going. For a while. Leon, think about it. What was there to wait around for, for so long? Don't you know by now that I am bad news for someone like you?

—Magda

P.S. Please don't write back. I'm doing the best I can. I don't think I could bear it.

Leon undid the clip from his belt loop and pulled his key ring out from under him. He fingered the mass of grimy keys one at a time, identifying each door in his many buildings: boiler, storage, supply, compactor, laundry, lobby, roof, elevator, car, office, shed, garage, toolbox, gate, alarm, mail. How he got in and out. Masterlock, Schlage, Medeco, QuikSet. The keys to the kingdom.

The sun had been so bright this morning as it fell

through the one window in his apartment that received direct light. Waking to it, his chest had crumbled beneath his skin, so powerful was the hopefulness of that light—the distance, the difference, between it and him. Each day it was harder and harder to get up. But the kingdom hadn't always needed keys. Once there was a time, you only had to be standing at its edge to feel it, like paradise; then, the doors, it seemed, were all open.

Just as, arriving home from P.S. 86, he would stand a long time in the archway of the living room awash in the walnut and emerald greens of reflected sunlight, watching his grandmother in the high-backed beige armchair. She wouldn't know he was there at first. Tree shadows waved like wheat across the purples and reds of the Persian rug and caressed her knees. In the bevels of the many small panes of window glass, rainbows shimmered, trapped. For Leon, this was like stepping out of the world into a realer world. On the wall in similar shadows hung a painting of a woman in a white dress holding with both hands the rope of a swing, dreaming the afternoon away. His grandmother was listening, her crooked spine held erect by the exquisite sorrow of the final aria of *Madame Butterfly*. Nothing could be more beautiful than someone dying with such a voice in this late afternoon light. Leon, sweaty and winded from the schoolyard, stood stopped in his tracks. He often woke at night to hear his grandmother groaning in pain and his grandfather telling her to shut her mouth, he needed his rest, before he got up to shift her onto her other side. Absorbed now into these lingering notes were her realer, lesser pains—her bent fingers that were like soft candles squashed against a wall. Each separate note was a polished diamond, glittering in the ear. Even Leon, as a boy, felt that. Here everything was changed. On the threshold of that room, holding his book bag like a forgotten trophy, Leon was struck by how smooth surfaces seemed, the curving panes of the hutch, the mirror above the mantle, the dusted table tops, and the shiny black facets of decorative coal in the fireplace. Madame Butterfly was on her knees now, hunched over, almost expired, changing herself into pure sound. He stood there so long, the shadow of the roof perceptibly inched across the carpeting. He waited for the final note and the echo of that note as it outlived the singer's death. In its aftermath, when he couldn't tell if the note still hung in the air or if it lived solely inside him, his grandmother would place a soft, gnarled hand beneath her chin and slowly shake her raised head. She was beautiful then. That was a kingdom her arthritis couldn't push its way into. The whole room seemed to be throbbing like a taste savored after the meal is over. Then a cultured, vaguely British voice intruded with seeming regret to announce the hour and what station they were tuned to. Leon's grandmother opened her eyes then and turned her silvered head toward him with pleasure as if she knew all along that he'd been there. It made the room his, and the music, too. He was let in on a secret all the objects in the room seemed to share. In the fading light, they radiated a rich intensity of earthy colors with which the room remained filled. Leon crossed into the room, now a part of it, under the aegis of his grandmother's smile, to lift the lid of the cut glass bowl on the oval coffee table and take out a piece of hard candy. He would untwist the colorful cellophane wrapper with its tiny picture of ripe fruit and suck it as they played gin rummy until night came on and he reached the tart, but soft, orange or raspberry center.

The arthritis tore her joints apart soon after that, and she couldn't even ride the wheelchair to the living room. She never had the radio brought to her. Had she asked his grandfather for it? Instead, the TV ran all day, a pharmacy of drugs beside her bed.

Roth hooked his keys back on his belt and stood up in the colorless light. He secured the kitchen cabinet doors, turned off the taps and glanced out the window at the snow. It was bluer now, like a bruise under the skin, nearer the end of day. Soon he would have to go. Roth went back to the bedroom for Bonforty's faucet. It wasn't there. It felt odd not to be holding it. He must have left it up in Melisandra Velarde's apartment.

aetana was standing by the elevator in the basement when it opened. His hair was beaded with snow. He smelled of garbage. "Mi'ta Rot'. You know those Indians in 6B, they say no heat coming up. Getting cold." Gaetana crossed his arms and patted his shoulders. He shook them like a dog shivering.

"The top floor gets the worst pressure, Edgar. And the boiler is off through the middle of the day."

"2D also complain. No heat."

"No heat or not enough heat?"

"No heat."

"Did you check to see? An air valve could be stuck shut."

Gaetana shrugged.

"3H also call, my wife say. No heat."

"Okay. I'll take a look. Meanwhile, the elevator. Did you notice? Someone's been using it for a toilet. It smells bad. It could use a mopping. You take care of that, and I'll check the heat."

Roth went down the steps into the boiler room. It had been dug to a deeper level than any room in the basement. The ceiling had a kind of cathedral height to it. The boiler itself had dimensions equally immense, its domed and orotund cast-iron packed with asbestos plaster. It looked like some of the giant mausoleums up in Woodlawn Cemetery. Armour, the hot dog family, had one like this. On its inside, the furnace with its chambers was like a heart. One chamber made steam; another made two thousand gallons of hot water; a third funneled exhaust up the chimney. The building was a shell without it. A corpse. Roth had always felt at home in this room with its vascular latticework of lines—oil, gas, waste, water—interlaced overhead and along the walls with a Rube Goldberg complexity.

Roth unlocked the door to the timer box. The time was correct, all the pins were in their places on the dial. The timer had clicked into its evening heat cycle, but the furnace hadn't fired up. Leon crossed the room to the oil tank. He wiped off the glass gage with his thumb. Just seventy-five gallons left. That was the note he'd forgotten to jot down on the roof. But still, the tank was low, not empty. Leon followed the line to the furnace. He unscrewed the cover of the oil filter; the screen was dirty but not too far gone. The tank must be thick with sediment, maybe forty years of it. Everything aged. You only knew it when something went wrong. Probably a gallon of sludge for each year of its existence. The kidneys filled with sludge, too, he'd read. Still, there ought to be at least thirty usable gallons left, unless the gauge was off. Leon hit the reset button. The burner fired up for a moment and then shut down. Leon went to the workroom and called for oil. Then he dialed the boiler man.

"Johnny? Leon Roth. Sorry to call you at home. But I've got an emergency. I've run low on oil at 162nd. The furnace keeps cutting out. Any chance you could get over here and take care of it? It's going to be a cold one tonight." Leon could hear him chewing. He chewed a long time. Leon heard him wipe his mouth. Four-forty. He'd gone home early today, and he was already eating.

"You're sorry, Leon? Well, I'm sorry too. I can't do it this evening. *Uuurrp.* Excuse me. I'll come by some time tomorrow. Teach that stupid spic to read the gauge, why don't you, instead of having to call me all the fucking time."

"This one was my fault, Johnny."

"Then you're a dumb spic, too, Leon."

"Can you get over here, first thing?"

"When I can, Leon, when I can. This ain't Porto Rico. Let 'em freeze their little butts off. Get a taste of the Northeast. It won't kill 'em." He belched again. "Hey! Get back to the table, you kids. I didn't say none of youse could get up yet. Hey, Garry, how many times I gotta tell you you can't give chicken bones to the dog. You're gonna kill him doing that."

Roth heard sounds of commotion. He swept the plastic shards of the plastic Jesus into his hand and tossed them behind the radiator.

"Jesus, Leon, kids—they're almost as dumb as tenants. Look, I'll be by tomorrow to clean up your mess. So long, Leon. And go home, Leon. There's nothing you can do about it."

In the boiler room Leon went over and touched the big two-inch pipe coming out the back. It was almost hot. They'd still have warm water for a while. What time had the burner shut down? It must be cold by now in the boy's bedroom in 4G. He'd be getting clammy in the armpits, between the legs. He'd pull his knees up and clasp his hands between his thighs. Maybe he'd moan a little. If no one were home yet, the cold would feel worse than being alone; he would feel like the last being alive.

Roth took off his coat and laid it on the ladder by the door. He found a bucket of kerosene back behind the boiler and cleaned the oil filter screen with it. Number six oil was normally thick as pudding; but this stuff was like a loose, fatty kielbasa. Magda's aunt had once served that to him. Even looking at it made him sick to his stomach. He had looked across the table to Magda for help, but she had grinned at his distress and with little squeaks of pleasure began eating her portion. It was clear to Leon that she hated it, too. So, Leon took a bite and mimicked her exaggerated delight. By turns, they complimented Magda's aunt, outdoing each other, suppressing giggles, managing to choke the sausage down. Her sweet, dumb aunt had beamed.

Roth scrubbed at the filter with a toothbrush he carried in his pocket. A sound like someone beating a metal drum with a stick racketed; the oil truck was delivering. He couldn't believe they had gotten there so fast. He went over to the gauge and watched the pointer climb. When it reached FULL the drumming stopped. Roth reassembled the filter. Then he removed the nozzle of the jet and cleared that out.

Roth cleaned himself off the best he could. Dark, oily stains had spread across his chest and above the knee. He wiped off the last of the kerosene from between his fingers and hit the reset button. The pump kicked in and a moment later the burner growled to life. Roth went to the ladder and put on his jacket. He'd go to the Chinese place on Fordham Road, Flor de Mayo, for the moo shu pork. He'd read the paper between bites, the endless dissolving news that floated like oil on the water of miseries and be perfectly anonymous amid the clatter of plates and shouted orders. He'd feel the pleasure of his fatigue, of this finality. He wanted to be alone, to be nobody, anybody, a mouth among mouths, chewing, swallowing, washing it down. He'd sip his Jasmine tea. He had done as Magda asked, not written. Every day since he'd gotten her letter he didn't write. Every day he was a mouth among mouths. Every day he bore it another day.

He thought of the boy in 4G growing warm and dry in his bed when the heat came back on. Maybe he'd even feel like getting up and having a bite to eat. Those oranges and who knew what other pungent stuff had gone into the beans. The boy would have some of that. It would heat his insides. He might even snicker if his brother knocked his glass of milk off the table. Gaetana would have the faucet back in by then. The last thing Roth would make him do. That was something, leaving things in working order. So that Morales's daughter could sit comfortably at her dinner table, electric with discontent. A burning bush, head to heel.

The burner shut off, the room fell silent. Roth hit the reset. It fired up then went off. He hit it again. Nothing happened. He smacked it. Nothing.

Roth sat down at the edge of the pit and listened to the ticks of the hot metal contracting as it cooled. It sounded like a countdown, as though something would happen on the last tick, an explosion, maybe, and blast him away. He wished it would. Something in him twitched with each tick.

"No rest for the weary, Leon. No rest for the weary." Alexander Lieberman stood on the top step. He looked vertiginously high from where Roth sat. Pushing back his hair, Lieberman came down the narrow steps sideways, as though following a goat path on a hillside, like some Moses way past his prime.

"Oy, Leon. First, it was the elevator, but that's okay—instead of bodily fluids, you smell Pine-Sol now. But such a concentration of pine! The super must have poured it on straight. That's a man who's always cutting corners. Frankly, the smell is stronger than piss, but at least you don't feel like gagging. But earlier, Leon, I felt a chill in the air, and now when I go to make a hot water bottle to put on Bea's neck—the neck is not doing so well—I'm no physician, Leon, but such a slender bridge between two such significant parts of the body, well, that's asking for trouble, it's a weak link in the species if you ask me. We have enough troubles without the neck acting up. Poor Bea, she can hardly move. I'm no medicine man, all I know is clothing, how to dress a neck, make it look good—did you ever look closely at a neck,

Leon? I have been observing Bea's neck this afternoon with great care, and I can say now with some authority the neck is not one of God's most comely creations, a hurried job in my opinion, not well thought out, he could have taken an extra day. After all, what was the rush? Who was counting?"

Lieberman made his way around the kerosene and sat down beside Roth. He swept his hair straight back off his forehead and fixed his eyes on the oil burner. "It's not working?"

Roth shook his head.

"I've never been in here before. So that's what's been doing the job for all these years. It's a real behemoth. Kaput?"

"No, tomorrow someone'll fix it."

"I see. We just have to get through the night. Is that it?"

"Tomorrow this building is going to have a new owner, Mr. Lieberman. It's being sold. Take my advice and start thinking about moving out."

"Selling? Why is Fein selling, Leon? It's still a good building. It's changed over the years, but who hasn't?"

"I don't really know. Business is business."

"Business is never just business. My partner used to say that to me when he was giving someone the shaft. That's why I got out. For me, it was also business, but never just."

Lieberman jumped to his feet, ran a hand through his hair and sat back down. Then he jumped up again. "And what are you going to do, Leon? Stay with Fein Realty?"

Leon shrugged.

"What do you want to do?"

Leon stared into the furnace. He could feel on his cheeks a small shimmer of heat still coming from the burner.

"You don't know? I see. You know, Leon, I got a call earlier today, from Betelman's wife. Widow, I should say. Betelman's dead. She tells me he died with a big, colorful scarf around his neck. Imagine that, I said. They can't figure it out. Poor Betelman! But Leon, that was a lucky man. He liked entering all those little numbers in his ledger book, he liked them to add up, come out even. Important, he felt. Keeping the world straight. That was

Betelman. It made life worth living for him, what my meshugganah brother used to call his 'ray zone debt.'

"Tell me, you got one of those, Leon? No, I can see you don't. It's hard without one. Me, Leon, I liked dressing people, putting them in clothes. It may not seem like much, but you can't imagine the good it did those men—checking the cut, the hang, in the mirror, doing their best to feel 'This is me.' With my help, they managed it most of the time. Frankly, there's nothing worse than nakedness, Leon. For men. They like their suits of armor. Numbers, clothes, cars. Women I don't know so well. Even Bea remains a mystery to me. In her pain, unable to move—just moments ago!—that woman set all the years aside and gave me a smile just like when we were first married. And I don't even know why. Poor Bea!"

Lieberman jumped up, tugged at the lapels of the yellow plaid sports coat he was wearing and started for the stairs. "I've got to get back. The dear girl will wonder where I am so long." He pulled himself up by the rail.

"Mr. Lieberman," said Roth. He imagined Lieberman's wife surfacing to smile above her pain like an old galleon that's been refloated, treasures in its hold. "Hot water isn't the answer. Your wife needs ice. An ice pack will make her neck better. You have to take down the swelling first. Heat'll only make it worse."

"This you know for a fact, Leon? Maybe you've missed your calling. A smart fellow like you should have been a doctor."

Lieberman stopped at the top of the stairs, winded. His wide red tie lay like a dog's tongue on his coat. He raised a hand to wipe back his hair, but it hovered, palm out, beside his face, instead, as though he were silencing a noisy crowd.

"Leon," said Lieberman, "I should set the record straight. It's not really so, what I said about my customers. They would try on trousers or a sports coat and look at themselves in the triple mirrors. They'd strike a pose and scrutinize all three versions of themselves. But they never said, 'This is me.' The clothes weren't them. No. They were trying to become the clothes. You see, they didn't know what they were until that three-piece suit told them.

Or until I told them it was a perfect fit. You know what my secret was? I'd frown and look concerned, withholding my approval until at least the third suit. All that getting into and getting out of. A man in his skivvies, Leon, is a sorry sight. That's what the dressing room is for. The hiding of embarrassment. Three times exposing their bony knees, and they were ready to be led. Those men were like putty in my hands."

Roth sat by the fire pit, still as the machinery, part of the inoperative boiler.

"What I'm driving at, Leon, is maybe you're not on your third change of threads yet, that's all. In the meantime, come up, why don't you, and tell Bea about cold and not hot. From me she won't hear it. After all, who am I? Just her husband of forty-eight years. I mean, are you planning to babysit this leviathan all night? Come! Talk with Bea. You she might listen to. You could make all the difference, all the difference in the world, Leon."

Landlord! Open the door!"

Roth could feel the persistent thudding through the walls. It felt like the sort of shaking that could bring this solid building tumbling down. He looked at his watch. It read five twenty-five. Obergon's eviction was going ahead. He was relieved not to be part of it. Again, he felt the heavy pounding, invasive, single-minded.

"Landlord! This is the landlord! Open up!"

The voice, unfamiliar to Roth, came through with sledge-like echoing shocks. Roth looked down at Lieberman's wife. She lay in bed like a large-winged bird broken by a fall, her head twisted on her shoulder.

"Open up! Open the door! Landlord!" Someone's fist now began jackhammering the door. The sound boomed through the walls.

"That's very loud, Leon. What's happening? Is someone knocking on our door?" Bea Lieberman turned her eyes up toward Leon. The skin on her cheek resembled tissue paper. He sat down on the edge of the chair by the bed so she could see him better. The bedspread which rose and fell with her breathing was the only thing that moved. The simplest movements caused her pain, she said.

"Even thinking," she had told him. "Can you imagine that, Leon? Even thinking hurts, but I'm afraid that's something I cannot stop doing." Her voice was remarkably calm, even curious.

"No, Mrs. Lieberman," replied Roth, trying to sound comforting, "those noises are coming from down the other end of the hall, 4A. It's nothing to worry about."

"Bea!" Lieberman called from the kitchen. Roth could hear him breaking ice from a tray. "I feel sure this is just the ticket. Leon is a quite the Renaissance man. He is knowledgeable about all manner of things. We'll have you up and about in no time, if not good as new, then as good as old."

Again the pounding. It sounded like a detonation cap going off. Roth tried to imagine what it must sound like from inside that apartment. Then another voice could be heard.

"Obergon! This is City Marshal Benvenuti. I have a warrant of eviction here in my possession. If you don't open the door and let us in, the locksmith will open it for us. One way or another we're getting in." Remarkable how clear, how penetrating it was. It felt as though the entire building were being evicted.

"Leon," said Lieberman's wife, "please don't let Alexander know. He really is a rather proud man. I think it has been very hard for him."

149 / THE MENSCH

Roth nodded.

Unbidden, this woman had told him she'd been madly in love once, before she'd married Lieberman, and that she had tried to take her own life.

"Sometimes, you know, Alexander looks at me askance, like the other night as I let the paper fall absently across my knee, and I knew he was wondering if it was on my mind, even after all these years, what happened with Nat and me. Mostly it's not, but I've been thinking about it today, about when we were young. God knows why. When you are flat on your back all day long, the mind goes in funny directions. And then, too, Leon, you remind me of Nat a little—that's why I felt like telling you—the way you mumble and turn your head away as you speak. Nat, from a discomfort with intimacy. But with you, it's from shyness, I suspect, isn't it?"

Roth shrugged.

She had never wanted something so much as she wanted this Nat character. When he jilted her, she simply made a decision.

"I was as calm about it," she said, "as I am right now. Calm and very lucid. Without this man, without what I felt for him, life, I realized, would be a paltry thing, indeed."

She was describing how she had calmly, lucidly slashed her wrists.

"It almost didn't have to do with Nat, not really. Alexander, I know, imagines that it's Nat himself, 'the love of my life,' I am thinking of. But that's not quite right, though I have never corrected Alexander on this score. I chose for passion, Leon. I sided with passionateness. Up till then, I had never really known it. And I have not known anything quite like it since. No, I was not desperate or lonely or terribly self-absorbed. I was no Madame Bovary. Actually, it was a glorious time. But I felt that to go on merely living would be a lesser thing, that's all, and what for, what would be the point once you knew what was possible? Why assent to a lesser thing, tell me?"

With an effort, she had tilted her head up then to look Leon in the eyes. "And, Nat, he wasn't even around much, you should know. He was in the service. He was what we called then 'dashing,' in appearance if not in manner. And no doubt he and I would have been very unhappy in the end. In fact, I believe, even then I actually spent more time with Alexander who lived just up the block from me. Alexander who even then always made me laugh. Why is it we don't take those who make us laugh as seriously as those who make us suffer? I have always thought that Alexander fell in love not so much with me as with the me that was so thrilled by being in love. Nat, I scarcely missed, it seemed, though I thought I did at the time. Everything was just so full, so poignantly full. I could hardly stand it. And then I knew it wouldn't be so full any longer, in just that way. And, as it turned out, I was right. Although there is no earthly reason for me to have been. But at times, even right now, for example, it feels as though I am very close to having been wrong."

Roth got to his feet as Lieberman came back in with the ice that he'd carefully crushed and inserted into the hot water bottle and wrapped with a hand towel.

"Thank you, Leon. Thank you. I can't thank you enough," he said, squeezing past Roth.

"Mr. Lieberman, don't thank me. I was wrong about what I said. Your wife needs a doctor, not ice."

"Thank you, Leon," Lieberman said, dismissing him. "I feel certain this will do the trick. Then Bea and I will get a little exercise, up and down the hall we'll stroll, and she'll feel like her old self, won't you, my love?"

Lieberman's wife smiled at him as he lowered himself by stages to his knees, beside her. Her eyelids fluttered in anticipation of pain, but she continued to smile, watching, Roth imagined, her husband's cartoonish concentration, inches away, as he searched for the exact spot to depress the mattress and insert the healing ice beneath her crooked neck.

To think that from the start he had been lovesick for her and had nursed, then coaxed, her back to willing life. A life's project. And that she had always let him think that this Nat was still in her heart, still his rival. That was the remoteness of her smile, Roth thought. She was smiling as though from some removed,

151 / THE MENSCH

true life toward her long second one with Lieberman. As though this life were a posthumous thing. And yet Lieberman seemed to touch and surprise her by his unflagging care and theatricality, even after all their years together. Was she the lucky one, or was he? Anyway, this second best life was the real one. There was ever only one life, however unreal it felt.

You might as well make something of your life, Leon. It sure as hell doesn't know what to make of you.

"How does this feel, my love?" he heard Lieberman say, as he went out the door. "Is it better this way? Or this?"

The hallway was crowded by the door to 4A. Roth could see Nimrud, the locksmith. Gaetana was there with two of his sons. Next to Benvenuti, the marshal, stood a large man in a long overcoat. Tenants milled against both walls. Roth looked back behind him toward the frosted windows at the empty end of the hall, dark as a movie screen. Roth approached the door as the stranger pummeled it again.

153

"Obergon, this is the last warning we're going to give. Open up if you know what's good," he bellowed.

Roth couldn't place the accent. Hakim was Lebanese, he'd heard, from Beirut, a city that had been even lovelier than the Bronx was, back in the 50s. A city of terraces, white and glittering on the shore of the Mediterranean. As many sorts of people as here. What would draw Hakim to a place like this? Roth watched Nimrud tip his head and whisper to Benvenuti. Both men began to laugh. Nimrud always told dirty jokes, particularly at evictions. Those were the only times he'd ever seen Nimrud in a good mood.

From inside, faintly, a woman's voice could be heard. The stranger snapped his fingers in the direction of Gaetana, gesturing.

"You, super, come over here. What's she saying?" He grasped Gaetana by the sleeve as he came over and tugged him in front of the door. The super put his ear carefully to it, like a safecracker. He squinted, whispering and nodding.

"Well, what's she say?"

"Obergon not home. She say to come back later."

"I don't care where Obergon is. You tell her to open the door." The man stepped forward and hammered again. "Tell her," he said.

A child began whimpering inside. Gaetana bent his head again. He spoke gently, with calm, as though to someone trapped in a mine. Then he turned to the stranger and held out the palms of his empty hands, apologetically.

That's what had always irritated Roth about Gaetana, that expectation of punishment. Now he saw why: Gaetana was sorry, sorry for everything in advance. But only because he expected to be blamed.

"She say her daughter is sick. She don't know where Obergon is. She say to come back tomorrow."

"Look, Gaetana, explain to her that it doesn't matter whether Obergon is here or in Timbuktu. If she doesn't have the five months rent, we are throwing her out of there. This isn't a charitable organization. Tell her," the stranger said, shoving the super's shoulder around to the door.

Nimrud snickered. Inside, the child was wailing. Roth could hear the mother clucking at the child to be quiet.

"Edgar, who is that woman?" Roth asked as he made his way forward. He had intended to stay just a moment, to catch a glimpse of Obergon as the force of law came down on his head. Now he came forward involuntarily. "Is she Obergon's girlfriend?"

"No, Mi'ta Rot'. This lady and her daughter move in, two, maybe three month ago. She give the rent to Obergon and he tell her he pay so there don't be no trouble. I tell her not to give him—he no give it to us—but she don't listen. He not in there. She say she can have some money by tomorrow."

"Are you Roth, Fein's outside man?" said the stranger, coming nearer, standing too close. "What are you still doing here?" He turned to the super. "Tomorrow's not good enough, tell her. Mr. Nimrud, it's time. Unlock the door."

Roth watched Nimrud drag his legs over to the door, the hinges on his metal braces squeaking at each step, a shrunken man with powerful arms. He gave Roth a sniggering smile, as if to say—you see, this is how it's done. At an eviction back in the fall, Roth had accepted a large, partial sum of money from the tenants and wouldn't let Nimrud lock them out. Something had told him to take the chance. He thought it wasn't just that he dreaded confrontations. Now Fein was back in court with them.

"You were supposed to be out of here. That was part of the deal," said the large man, turning to Roth. Close up, Leon could smell the remains of cologne, Brut or something like it, a rancid, aggressive odor. "What deal? The closing's not till later. If anyone's trespassing here, it's you." Roth stared into the dark, hairy face that for the first time turned its full attention on him.

"You're not needed here, Roth. We're taking care of this now." Small, narrow eyes that didn't blink seemed to size him up as though he had been the object of prior conversation. Had Fein been talking about him? Roth had never considered what Fein thought of him before. Was there some allegiance among landlords that took precedence over other loyalties?

"So take care of it, then," Roth replied. The man was breathing heavily through his nose. Roth made a show of looking around him. "But I don't seem to see any movers here, Mr. Hakim. Where are they?"

"Everything goes in the basement, it's cheaper that way. If this Obergon fellow wants his stuff, he can pick it up there. My name's Adjani, by the way, not Hakim. I work for Mr. Hakim. God knows why you're still here, Roth, but since you are, why don't you stick around after. You can show me a few things."

"Bingo," said the locksmith straightening up. "That's lock number one. Am I good, or what?" He readjusted his legs and bent over the lower lock.

Roth wondered if the woman inside was still there by the door, watching the latch turn as Nimrud worked it from the outside. When the door opened, she would be dispossessed. Nothing but what she could carry would belong to her anymore. Did she know this was about to happen?

"You people," ordered Adjani, pointing to the tenants in the hallway, "back up, please, you're going to be in the way standing there."

The second lock gave, and the marshal went in first, carefully, just in case, with the warrant in his hand. The woman had been standing by the door all along, it seemed; now she backed up into the apartment, the child in her arms, sobbing. The woman was small, slight; she kept having to tug the girl higher.

Benvenuti towered over her. "Are you Mrs. Obergon?"

The woman shook her head. Roth could see that she was bewildered and frightened. Adjani pushed past them, the super and his sons right behind him.

"You're going to have to leave, ma'am. The landlord is taking possession of the apartment for non-payment of rent. Gather up the things you want to take with you. You'll have to go." She began talking to the marshal, but he shrugged. "I'm sorry," he said. "*No hablo Español.*"

Adjani's harsh, loud voice echoed from inside the apartment. "Okay. Everything in here goes. I want you to get it all out in the hall first. Pile it up out there by the elevator. Hey, Nimrud!"

"Yes, Mr. Adjani."

"Go ahead and change the lock cylinders. Save the old ones for me. And let me have both sets of the new keys.

"You, super, once everything is out of here, take it to the basement and put it in storage. You don't open that door for nobody, understand? Obergon wants his stuff, you have him call me. Got that? Okay. Start in the bedroom."

The woman had withdrawn into the doorway of the kitchen. Listlessly, her eyes followed the pieces of furniture and armfuls of clothing as they were carried past into the hallway. The child clung to her neck, but she didn't seem aware of it. Most of the tenants were leaving. Nothing interesting was going to happen, no argument, no fight. A few remained to examine what the super and his sons were carting out.

"Look, lady," said the marshal, "I wouldn't be standing there if I were you. You should be packing." He mimed placing things into a suitcase.

The woman just stood there. She didn't seem to hear him or understand his gestures. She watched the super's two boys stagger out with a mattress.

"Hey, lover boy." Melisandra was standing beside Leon. "You forgot this." She pushed the faucet into his hands. "From downstairs I heard all the noise. What gives?"

"Obergon's being evicted."

"Obergon? He doesn't live here. He left months ago."

The two boys carried out a dresser, bumping first against the doorknob, then the door jamb.

"Easy with that! Easy!" Benvenuti hollered. He had out a clipboard and was taking inventory.

"Where are they moving these things?" Melisandra asked.

"They're putting Obergon's things in the basement."

"These things aren't Obergon's. They belong to Inés. All of it does."

"It's Obergon that's being evicted. Who is this woman? I've never seen her before."

"What's it matter who she is, Leon? You can't throw a woman with a small child out on the street." Melisandra took her eyes off a large mirror Gaetana's boys were carrying through the door. "Tell them to stop, Leon. You're the agent here."

"I can't stop it. It's too late to stop it now. This woman's got no legal right to the apartment."

"So you're just going to toss her out in the snow because she hasn't got a legal right? I happen to know that she's got nowhere else to go."

"What can I do?" Leon pleaded. He lifted his hands the way Gaetana had. "Even if it were up to me, I couldn't let her stay. Her name's not on the lease."

"You're not helpless, Leon. Figure something out."

"What am I supposed to do? Until ten minutes ago, I didn't even know she was living here. As far as the law's concerned, she doesn't even exist. It's out of my hands."

"Mr. Pontius Pilate, I almost forgot. You're one of these people, aren't you, Leon? All that sweet talk about nature and stuff didn't mean jackshit, did it? Maybe you think this is different? You think cause this is business, you're off the hook. Well, you're not. It's all hooked together, Leon."

She turned away from him toward the open door and began slapping her hand against her thigh. "Damn, damn, damn! I told Inés to call the landlord and tell them she was living here now." She pointed her finger at Leon. "Leon the peon. I got to tell you. You're one big disappointment." She pushed into the apartment past the super, who was dragging out a rolled-up rug. Roth looked down at the faucet in his hands. He rubbed its peeling spout. It felt as though it belonged under his arm. Battered, it looked to him like a bird with its wings clipped.

As he unlocked the door and pushed in, Roth could hear voices coming from the inner offices in the back. A gust of snowy wind blew in with him. Fein Realty had its office in a storefront on Gun Hill Road in a building that belonged to another realtor. "My God," Fein had said, "there'd be no end to interruptions if we were housed in one of our own buildings. We'd get nothing done. Nothing! All day tenants would be trooping through complaining that the brass isn't polished, that their apartment is too hot or too cold. We'd go out of our minds."

The voices were coming from Fein's office, the largest. Voices meant that they hadn't started the closing yet or that the legalities were just over. It had taken Roth a long time to get back. The Chevette had gotten stuck in the snow as he pulled out of his parking spot. The string of street lamps glowed in the still heavily falling snow as dimly as lights in a coal mine. Beacons, nevertheless. Along the Concourse cars were stalled and aimed in every direction like a wall of clocks all keeping different time. He couldn't seem to feel the road beneath his wheels, as though his tires weren't really in contact with the ground. He remembered reading in some physics textbook that no object actually ever touched any other: touch was just an illusion. The example was a billiard ball, which for all it seemed to kiss off or collide with other balls, never, in fact, did. It wasn't mechanical energy that drove them apart. There was some kind of force field—you never got closer to anything or anyone than an atom's width. As Leon fishtailed up Jerome Avenue, that space gaped wide as the space between stars.

Leon stamped the snow off his feet, hung up his parka and went over to his desk. From down the hall he could hear Fein's voice slicing above the others like a reciprocal saw biting in. Until now Roth had admired Fein's ability to take charge of a conversation. It was never Fein who got cut off mid-sentence, never Fein who deferred when someone else began speaking at the same time. Those who didn't have this force of personality always seemed grateful to those that did. Roth, too, was guilty of this. Before, Leon had thought this characteristic of Fein's a consequence of having a zealot's conviction. Now he felt it—the exclamations, the accusations, the rhetorical questions, the volubility—as a need to dominate, to assert pride of place.

Fein's drone was punctuated by laughter, and Roth guessed that Fein was regaling those assembled with the story that Eddie,

Fein's handyman and a tough character, had told them last week. When he'd lurched into the office that day, he looked like he'd been struck by lightning, mute and disheveled. Since then, Fein had been telling the story to anyone who'd listen.

"Glazing a windowpane in this apartment over on University, something, some large thing, out of the blue, drops onto Eddie's head and shoulder. Eddie, who's terrified of spiders, thinks a giant hairy tarantula has glommed onto him, though Eddie has never in his life seen more than a picture of one. It's like a real life horror movie and suddenly he's starring in it. He leaps up and starts running around the bedroom, whacking with the hammer that's in his hand, half the time whacking himself in the head. A good thing Eddie has such a hard one. But the thing hangs on and Eddie lunges about the apartment shrieking, flailing at it, running into walls, bookshelves, floor lamps, you name it, he knocks it over. This is our cool-under-fire Eddie I'm talking about. Finally he makes it to the door and makes his escape. Alone. The thing is gone. But he tears down the street to his car anyway and starts driving. Oy, Eddie! He's forty miles out of the city, up the Thruway and over the Tappan Zee bridge before he comes to and pulls over. Can you believe it, forty miles? The only reason he stops is that he runs out of change for the toll booths. A week goes by, he still doesn't go back for his tools or his jacket. I have to send Raphael over there for his stuff. The thing on his back, it turns out, was a monkey. A monkey of all things! And it also turns out that Eddie brained it to death. Eddie, our resident animal lover. So, what am I going to do? There's no law against monkeys. Though let me tell you, if I knew this guy had a monkey on a string, I'd never in a million years have rented him the apartment. So I agree to pay for the shattered knick-knacks, the busted bookcase, everything Eddie broke. But when it comes to the monkey, I draw the line. I tell the tenant, get this, 'You'll have to take me to court. I'm not going to have that monkey on my back.'"

It always ended, like a punch line, with the same phrase. Fein relished it. Each time he got to the end of the story, he'd repeat it. "Now, at least, our happy-go-lucky, no-thought-for-tomorrow

Eddie knows what it's like to have a monkey on his back. Jesus, a monkey!"

Roth had heard it so often he knew it by heart. Each time he thought about the monkey, bludgeoned by the hammer.

And Eddie. Leon hadn't thought of him all day. With anyone else a scene like that would have remained a comedy; with Eddie it always turned into a tragedy. What made it turn out that way? The need to hurt? To make someone pay? Eddie never knew when to stop. Short, ferret-like, with pimples that had tiny white heads, even on his forehead, manifold as the light bulbs on a movie marquee. When he talked to you, he stood way too close, like Adjani.

Eddie would frequently show up Monday mornings with bruises on his face and say, grinning, "It was him or me, him or me. What was I supposed to do?" That was tragedy: either/or. Eddie was like a defective instrument that could play only two notes. Did any instruments do only that? Maybe two strings, but not two notes. Everything was primitively personal with Eddie. When he smiled, it meant: Just wait, I'll get you for that.

Fuck him, thought Leon, slamming closed a desk drawer; it made a tinny, sheet-metal sound. And fuck Fein, too, for keeping Eddie around. But Eddie was useful, he would have been down there for the eviction if Fein wasn't selling the building. Well, fuck useful. Leon took the rent monies Edgar had given him out of his notebook and tossed the notebook in the wastepaper basket.

A voice Leon couldn't place now bubbled up over Fein's. Was it Hakim's? His lawyer's? In its own way, this voice was like Fein's. Sharp, spasmodic, guttural, sounds like you heard pressing your ear to the fleshy softness of a stomach—farts and bubblings, percolating, squeezing and flapping sounds. Thinking or speaking: maybe those were just another kind of biologic life. What he was hearing was nothing but the farts and gurgles of social life.

Leon rubbed his cheek, feeling its prickliness. He rolled a lease agreement into the carriage of the typewriter. He backdated it, typed in Inés Felix's name, apartment 2F, made it a three-year, put in the rent figure, rolled it out, signed his name, her name, and paper clipped it to an envelope into which he slipped Obergon's five hundred-dollar bills and placed it carefully under other papers on Ellen's desk. She'd find it in the morning and enter it into the roll. He could imagine Melisandra saying to him, *You may be a Samaritan, Mr. Do Nothing, but there's nothing good about it.*

It was something, anyway.

Again, laughter. This time Fein's and the stranger's loudest. Doing business. An Arab and a Jew. Laughing together. Maybe that's what was needed to solve the Arab-Israeli conflict. Poor people. You could ship half the Bronx to Gaza, and Nimrud, too. Give the Israelis and Palestinians a joint partnership. You'd see how successfully they could work together having blacks, Jamaicans, Dominicans, and Puerto Ricans to make their living off. Just give them some people even more alien than they are to each other.

Nobody likes to see themselves mirrored when they look at someone else. You, Leon, are so out of it that when you look in the mirror not even then does anything look familiar.

Had Magda once said that to him? Or was it just the kind of thing she would likely have said? Well, fuck Magda, too. It's not just me that's out of it. The Bronx, the whole fucking world, is out of it. Only the unfamiliar looks familiar. When you let a cage of rats overpopulate itself, the rats don't think it's getting too crowded, that someone's experimenting with them. No, instead, they just start taking a dislike to those rats closest to them as if they were to blame. Soon, they're snarling and biting each other, eating their own children. Christ, thought Leon, as he listened to chairs scraping across the floor of Fein's office, maybe I should go in and join them. I'm just one of the rats, after all, aren't I?

Instead, he swivelled back and forth, gazing at the clutter on his desk, a twisted brass hinge, a moisture detector, paint samples. On top of some stapled receipts and a hardware catalogue lay a thick packet. Ellen must have put it there when she realized he wasn't coming in. The handwriting was familiar. Leon picked it up. Serce, it read, and under it the return address gave the nuthouse Magda had been in, in her hand. Postmarked just two days back. Was she returning his letters? He swivelled away.

The past. If you really wanted to get beyond it, you couldn't leave bits of it around. Holding onto souvenirs indicated that you couldn't let them go. It probably even meant more than mere attachment; it meant you yearned for it back. Therefore: burn your bridges; tie yourself to the mast; ship cargo; bail. Whatever it takes.

Maybe Magda just wanted to make this clear, in case her letter hadn't. Just in case the affection Leon detected in its tone might be mistaken for an invitation. Leon felt like a contagion. Magda stuffing his letters into the mailer while pressing a handkerchief to her mouth and nose. He felt like something being cut out, a ruptured appendix or tumor. Leon swivelled back and rummaged for his letter opener and carefully slit open a seam and read.

Dear was-Leon, once Leon, once upon a time Leon, erstwhile Leon, fragment Leon, used car Leon, prior Leon, prepost Leon, fossil Leon, mumbling Leon, Pre-Cambrian Leon, bygone Leon, previous Leon, old-growth Leon, Leon the ruin, Leon the Leon, figment of his former Leon.

Leon turned the page.

Dear Leon, dear half-life Leon, expletive deleted Leon, dismantled Leon, continental drift Leon, Brezhnev Leon, eonsago Leon, lost Leon, long-lamented Leon, Leon who left me, Leon who never calls Leon, forgotten by Leon, lack Leon, lepidopterous Leon, lapsed Leon, immemorious Leon, sedimented Leon, fair-weather Leon, failed Leon.

Leon turned the page.

Dear, dear Leon who I loved, Leon who I loathed, inert Leon, mute Leon, motherless Leon, little orphan Leon, Leon salvatious, Leon the led, clueless, occluded Leon, receding

Leon, Leon the sponge, the spongy, nothing to nobody, lots to little Leon, tepid, tenacious Leon, lackluster Leon, dwindling Leon, dissolving Leon, Steppenwolf Leon, step'n fetch it Leon, eggs in one basket Leon, carry on Leon, carrion Leon, decayed Leon, withered, petered out, finite, used up, dried out Leon, unrenewable Leon, lightless Leon, loveless Leon, once-loving unlovely, guttering Leon,

The salutations ended. The following page was blank. Well, par for the course. Nothing ever followed. It all led right to the cliff edge. Leon flipped the pages, one at a time. On the ninth page the letter began.

This is how it goes: my parents come to see me. I am a virtual Buddha, erect, motionless. My mother paces, she twists something in her hand, a hankie, a scarf, her hat. Well, how are you, she asks in a thousand hesitant hoping ways. I wait. I just wait. Then it comes. My father, as if in anticipation, slides the box of chocolates surreptitiously onto the dresser as my mother works herself up. All that's missing is a get-well card with it, as if I'm in to get my tonsils out. What's happened? she begins, like clockwork. It's automatic as if she were going through Mass. What's happened to you, you used to be such a, such a, such a, … etc.

And this is how it goes: the shrink comes to see me. He says, you are using your anger as a weapon. It is a strategy to keep yourself here. You are going to have to admit it, you want to be here, you want to! Etc.

And this is how it goes: all those letters that came instead of you. The past wasn't good enough, you had to retouch it like a photograph. You had to turn it into something else.

My mother is rewriting what I was like.

The shrink's rewriting what I want.

And now you've rewritten what we were.

I can't move! I can't breathe! No one will let me be!

My uncle Teddy is the only one I let visit me now.

He's just like the rest of them, deep in the cave, but he has to belch through the hole in his throat in order to speak. It's a terrible sound, and he has to work at it as though he were trying to play a broken trumpet. He sits there with tears in his eyes. All I can think is that he must have swallowed his cancer, that it's lying in his hard swollen gut like radioactive waste, growing larger and larger.

So: Teddy sits opposite me on a hard metal chair, and he's dying. He's dying and he's pleading with me like a bullfrog. Uncle Teddy, I say, oh, Uncle Teddy. He's dying yet he's doing his best to make me feel bad, as though the life being ruined is my mother's. A loyal emissary. Uncle Teddy, I say, and tears come to his eyes. He thinks he's gotten through to me, that I want to be a good girl, but that somehow I can't, that I'm a victim, too, just like my mother, a victim of myself. He burps up more words and we sit facing each other now with tears in both our eyes. He's a big, dumb brute of a man, but that wobbling flap of skin at his trachea which he forgets to cover makes all the difference to me, makes it awful, makes it okay.

You find out you're dying, Leon, like the rest of us, come see me.

My anger is my own. Pure me. That's why they want me to give it up. The moment it's gone, I'll be dead, down in Uncle Teddy's stomach. Then they'll give me the *Good Housekeeping* seal of approval.

You reimagined the past for me, Leon. Well, in return I reimagined the present for you. To get you to stop with the letters. Vengefully at first. And cleverly. Then nobly. But we know about nobility, don't we? The secret is: it's a selfish form of sacrifice. A way to get one's way. Needy. Ignoble to its rotten core. Either way, it's just no good. Noble, needy: you're on your own. You can't fool them. You can't fool them. You see that, don't you? All those Leons. All those decent little Leons. I'm sorry, Leon. It's just not up to me to let you off the hook.

Leon turned the page; there were many more of them, as many as the pages he had sent Magda, but it, and the others, as he rapidly shuffled them, turned out to be blank. No name. No signature. No mark. Leon ran his eyes over each one, back and front, as if they contained invisible handwriting or a meaning that was hard to make out.

He stared at them as at a movie screen when the house lights come up. All day, he had tried to bring to mind the end of *Old Yeller.* He had a nagging suspicion that he was misremembering it. The more he thought about it the less clear it got. The rabies had turned the loyal dog into a hostile stranger. Like it had never known the boy. He could see that. Then it struck him. The father hadn't shot the dog at all. The boy had done it. Had the father made the boy do it? "It's your dog, son. A man's got to take responsibility for what's his." Some malarkey like that so that the boy would kill a piece of himself? That was the key, the price of the ticket. A piece of yourself. "Welcome to the club, son. Now you're one of us." Another seal of approval.

It had gone silent in the other room as though no one were in there, as though a tape recording of voices had been left to run out. Whatever they were doing, he wasn't part of it. He would go in to them in his own good time. He would go in when he remembered how the movie really ended.

Leon could see now the stones the boy and his sister were piling up on top of the dog's grave. The father had only returned afterwards, with a pony for his son. The father hadn't made the boy do it. The boy had insisted on doing it himself. Love. Ownership. Necessity. That's what was behind it. The whole thing was long in the making. How had he gotten it all so wrong? And the boy's mother. She was in this somehow, too, nearby, seeing it through, behind the scenes. The yellow light on everything. It wasn't the sun or the dog or the terrain. It came from the boy's mother, her skin, her hair. Unspeaking, but present. All the more present for not being there.

And finally, after it was over, there it was: the puppy to take Yeller's place. That final nail in the coffin: the accepting of a substitute. Of one thing for another. Time's dirty little secret. Leon went through the unwritten pages one more time. He couldn't find a trace of himself or Magda in them.

The door to Fein's room opened, voices again now loud and distinct, the words audible, as though Roth suddenly were able to understand a language previously foreign to him. It was so often disappointing to know what people were actually saying. So much less interesting than you imagined. People often had such small concerns which they treated with the grave intensity of large ones. Edgar and his compactor bags. Fein and his rents. Whether Teflon tape or lampwick worked better on pipe threads—all argued with utter conviction. Small thoughts, large feelings. Better to listen and not understand the words. The feelings were grand. That was the thing about passions, they were independent, like ghosts waiting to inhabit some dead or somnolent body. Passion. It was always looking for a pretext. It was like the city reservoir springing leaks from a weak joint or loose coupling. Leon could feel behind his eyes terrific pressure like in the pipes. Pressure. It pushed evenly in all directions, tireless, testing. Opening the tap didn't even relieve it.

Fein's large squared-off head and the tips of his fingers emerged sideways from around the corner of the hallway. "Finally, Leon, you make it in. No one sees you all day. But now, when there's nothing to do here, you've come. Why you've bothered, I'll never know. All day you've bothered with the wrong things. Where is your sense of priorities? Where?"

Fein stared at Roth with those bulging, hypnotic snake eyes. The frozen look of penetration, judgment. Roth had always felt transfixed by this look, pinned as if to a dissecting board. Now it struck him that Fein's wet, unblinking eyes didn't see him at all. They were just a symptom of an illness. Fein's Passion. Priorities. Good Business Sense. "Grow up," Fein had said to him. "This is the way the world works."

The thing is, Leon, they just want to turn us all into pets. If you're good, you can have all the kitty litter you'll ever need.

That was Magda's passion. And what was his? What was his?

Fein's eyes still on him, Roth turned back to his desk as though he were busy and slit open the first thing he could find, an over-sized Publisher's Clearinghouse mailer. "You could already be a winner!!!" it read.

There was a knock at the front door, and Fein, the spell broken, lunged to open it. "Okay, okay, it's about time!" he barked into the face of the delivery boy. Roth could hear the crinkling of paper bags, Fein poking around in them to make sure everything was there. No detail too small. "Okay, okay," he said, "keep the change, sonny."

On Roth's desk, Fein went through the food again. "The closing should have been over by now, but the fact is, Leon, you're in time, we're just starting. I ordered some take-out. There's a lot of fine print to go over. Ha! Fine print! Get it? It's going to be a while until we're through. I ordered you some of that eggplant shit you like. Am I clairvoyant, or what? So, stop putzing around and get your butt in there. And, Leon, move that damn faucet out of the way before someone trips over it."

He was a good kid, a mensch. *Mensch*, officer. That's a Yiddish word. It means—what?—a good egg. A decent person. Someone who keeps his promise, someone you can count on, who thinks of others. Decent. More than decent. It's funny, though. No one likes to be called one. Roth didn't. I don't think he liked the fact that he was one. Somebody calls you a mensch, you tend to hear a smirk or taunt in it, like they're making fun of you. Someone says mensch and you hear, loser. You hear, sucker, mama's boy, kiss-ass, milksop. You want to kick 'em in the teeth for saying it. But you're a mensch. So, you don't. You just swallow it. And you remember, because a mensch remembers. You, Sergeant, you're probably one yourself. Or you would have been. But you're a Mick. Anyone not in your family, you'll put the screws to them, if need be. No qualms. Am I right? A mensch, the poor bastard, he has qualms all over the place. He doesn't know where or how to stop having them. I mean when he first comes in, what does this Roth do? Even though the building's changing hands, and, by agreement, we're not responsible anymore? He's rented an empty apartment, and he's writing out a lease. Puts five hundred bucks in an envelope, first and security. Frankly, he could have stuck it in his pocket. But here it is. Ines Felix, 2F. It's not his problem anymore, but he's a mensch, so it is his problem. He may not even want to do it, but he can't help himself. He may feel bad doing it, but he feels worse if he doesn't. You can see why a mensch doesn't like being called one. There's no pleasure in it. It's a burden, a kind of curse. Like being born with a bit in your mouth instead of a silver spoon. I consider myself lucky it didn't happen to me. My old man used to slap me silly. I've got a lot of fuck-you in me. Your old man wallop you, McNamara? You're probably a real son of a bitch, too. Well, that's a good thing. You're you, and I'm me. We don't ever forget who we are. A mensch has a hard time with that one. You got a problem? Well, tough, it's yours, you solve it. Hey, I'll listen to your troubles. But, you know what, the bottom line is, they're yours. They get in the way of your work, watch out. I'm not going to sympathize. I'm going to ream your ass. I was fortunate Roth was the mensch type. Mensches tend to be eager beavers. You give them a pat on the head. You toss them a bone once in a while. They work their asses off. A mensch likes to please.

"The son of a bitch! I didn't know if he carried a weapon. I advise all my people against it. It's false security. It's more likely to get you hurt. A threatening situation you can talk your way out of. Pull out a gun or a knife, and anything can happen. But, look, managing property's a dangerous job. You are not beloved out there. You are not going to win any popularity contests. And half the time you've got rent money fattening your pockets. So it's understandable. But still, a letter opener! This whole situation's just unbelievable! I just can't take it in that it's happened! It beggars the imagination. What was he thinking? What was he thinking!

"No, Roth may not have had any balls, but he was a walking pressure cooker just the same. Maybe it was my fault. Well, partly my fault. I was always turning up the flame. I'd bust his chops about the small things, and if I was particularly ticked off I'd needle him, 'Come on, Leon, come on! Be a mensch! Be a mensch!' I could tell it got under his skin. Almost nothing seemed to, that's why I did it. You've got to be annoyed in this business, on edge. Bare your teeth if people don't come through. You've got to get inside their heads. Make them worry about what you'll do or say. Roth never got angry. Irritable, yes. But I wanted him to explode now and then. I worked at him. I made him a kind of project. I thought, let him explode at some tenant or the plasterer when the guy fucks up, so the next time he'll think twice. Who knew it would happen this way, that he was such a crazy son of a bitch? This afternoon, he got pretty exercised over the phone when I told him we were selling this building on 162nd Street and closing on it this evening. That surprised me. Normally, there'd be a long silence on the line. I never liked that silence of his. Something about it always gave me the feeling that he was criticizing, judging me, that he didn't like the way I did things. Who did he think he was, the little twerp! He didn't build this business, I did. This afternoon, when he began complaining, it surprised me. I jumped down his throat. His throat. That's a laugh.

"What happened? From the beginning? Let's see. We were all in the room. The lawyers were at the desk, in front and in back, Mr. Hakim and I were on either side of it, and Eddie was behind us by the window, eating. Roth sat by the door over there. He didn't say anything. He was holding this dumb kitchen faucet in his lap, working away at the handles, tightening, loosening, I don't know what. To be honest, it was getting on my nerves. They squeaked. Every few minutes, I'd turn to him and say, would you quit it with that thing? It was distracting all of us. There we were reading through the contract, line by line, clarifying this and that, making sure nothing's left out. Before you know it, he'd start up again, twisting and squeaking. I figured the kid could learn something being there. But as far as I can tell, he wasn't paying the least bit of attention. Even Eddie, who doesn't have a clue about these things, seemed interested, was following along.

"Then, Hakim's outside man, a Mr. Adjani, who was down at the building, as per our arrangement, called to say that the boiler wasn't working. Lots of consternation around the table, you can imagine. A potential land mine. We call people. The lawyers get busy writing in some new language about who's liable for what. I apologize to Hakim about the boiler. Meanwhile Roth, he's just sitting there playing with those handles as though he were making careful, fine adjustments on some sort of delicate instrument, you know, an oscilloscope or something. When we have this thing pretty much straightened out, Hakim says to Roth something like, 'Thank you, Mr. Roth, for getting us off to such an auspicious beginning. My agent tells me you were there until a short while ago and didn't bother to inform him about this problem.'

"It's nerves, you see. I'm a little surprised at Hakim. But the fact is, a closing isn't just a formality. It's fraught. Somewhat momentous. From here on out everyone's lives are going to be different. The future is an anxious blank. I've been through lots of them. At a closing, everyone's giving off sparks. But Hakim is a gentleman. He reminds me of David Niven. Cultured. Maybe it's his accent and his precise English. Anyway, he knows how to inflict a wound without drawing blood. I have to say I admire that.

"But before I have a chance to say anything, Roth, who often has some wise ass, sarcastic comeback on his tongue, says, 'Anything I can do to help, Mr. Hakim. Maybe you'd like me to go back and wreck the elevator for you, short out some fuses. Why wait for neglect to take care of it. I mean, look at what you people are doing to Beirut. I've seen pictures. That's not neglect. That's effort, isn't it? Have you come here to the Bronx for a little target practice? What did the Bronx ever do to you to deserve your attention?'

"Roth gets up, takes a step toward Hakim and throws the faucet into his lap. 'Here,' he says, 'this is yours, too. 4G. It's broken. You might want to put it back in. On second thought, why bother? Those people, they're just infidels, right? When you're not salaaming to Mecca, you probably spend your time devising new ways to screw them over, or maybe that's what you do while you're praying. I bet it helps pass the time.'

"Now I'm too stunned to get up, but Hakim has jumped to his feet like the faucet was red hot. He flings it to the floor. There's a tear in his pants where the metal had dug in, and he's rubbing his thigh. It's amazing how calm his voice is, although his face tells a different story, and he says, 'We're Maronites, Mr. Roth, not Muslims. We don't regard ourselves as Arabs, but Phoenicians. And as for Beirut, which, sadly, you don't seem to know the first thing about, my family, no doubt like yours, has long been residing here in this country.'

"Roth pulls out what looks like a knife and sneers. It seems theatrical, like play-acting, it's so out of character. I mean, the whole thing is unbelievable, a nightmare in the making. 'Phoenicians, my foot,' he sneers, 'ass-fuckers is what you are, Hakim. Sodomites. Faggots. *Maricones*. That's what your new tenants are going to call you, you scumbag, not Phoenicians.'

"Hakim, like I indicated, is an elegant, dapper man, slight, delicate even. It all goes with the nice manners, the uncreased suit. But the look he gave Roth then said it all. He was trembling and rigid. There was murder in his eyes. The last thing you'd want to do was cross someone like that. If Hakim had had a gun on him, he would have shot Roth, consequences be damned. Roth pushed about every button there was to push except maybe to call his wife a whore.

"I should've pushed Roth right out the door, right out of the office, right onto the street and locked him out. But I began yelling—this was a catastrophe, after all. If only he'd waited a little longer, till everything was signed, I would have told him to shut up, apologized profusely to Hakim, and that would have been that. If only he'd called it a day, gone home, instead. If only. But here we are, nothing's signed, the boiler's busted, and it looks like it's all going to fall through, and we're back at square one. So I start yelling, partly to shift the attention off of them and onto me, and I step in between them.

"'What do you think you're doing, who do you think you are,' I tell Roth, backing him up. 'Get out of here, I won't stand for this behavior. I won't put up with you any longer, you're fired. You're fired!' I say it again. I want to make sure everyone has heard it clearly. I'm upset, but I'm also trying to salvage this thing. 'Go!' I yell, 'pack your things! Clear out your desk! Get lost!'

"Roth is right at the door now, as good as gone, so I turn back now to massage Hakim. He's still got this fierce, animal suspicion on his face, as though Roth has voiced what all of us were thinking, as though it is just dawning on him that the primary fact is that he's buying this building from Jews. He probably even imagines Eddie is a Jew. I see that I've got my work cut out for me. It's going to take a lot of sutures to stitch this wound back together. Deepsixing Roth isn't enough. I'm going to have to ostracize him, cut him away from us, pollute him.

"'I should have gotten rid of him a long time ago,' I say. 'He's bad news. It was as a special favor to his grandfather that I took him on. I've bent over backward to honor my obligation. Now I'm sorry, truly sorry, that I was so patient with him. He's a bad egg.'

"For all I'm saying, though, I'm already forgetting about Roth, the little prick. He's the past. This is business. The whole thing is hanging by the thinnest thread. I'm walking toward Hakim, I've got my arms out to help him back to his chair, minister to his leg, ask his forgiveness, whatever it takes, when someone's got me tight around the throat, dragging me backwards. I can't draw breath, I'm gasping for air. I don't know what's going on. I'm staggering back caught in this strong grip, and then I'm being tripped down into a chair. My head goes back, it's being crushed against a belt buckle, and looking up is when I first realize it's Roth who's doing this. I see this silver flash, the knife he's pulled out, and he's got me under the chin, pulling up hard but gently, the way a barber does to stretch the skin of the neck before he starts shaving it. I'm staring right into Roth's face now, and I feel the blade pressing against my throat, and to be honest, I'm not thinking of anything, remembering anything, planning anything. I'm not praying either, I'm just looking up into the black, lima bean-shaped openings of his nostrils. He's breathing heavily through them onto my face. Maybe God comes later, McNamara, or it's only at the very last instant that the past flashes before your eyes, I don't know. But right then, there are just those nostrils, moist and black and the black is so black it's disgusting. I'm scared shitless, to be honest, and I'm bleating, 'Leon, Leon, Leon.' Nothing else comes out. Like it's the first word or the only word.

"'Shut up, Allan,' he says, 'quiet down.' He says it tenderly like I'm a kid who's afraid of something which he knows won't hurt. He looks as though it's going to hurt him more than it will me; it's as open and friendly and concerned a face as I've ever seen on him. Here he's about to slit my throat, and I'm overcome with feeling, touched that I never knew he liked me so much and surprised that it seems to matter and that I want him to. Isn't that weird? We stay that way a long time, it seems. I don't know where any of the others are, and that doesn't seem to matter either. Maybe one of them makes a move, I don't know. Then, slowly, cradling my face, he draws the blade across my windpipe, and when it's done, he screams. I screamed, too, I think. If it was anything but that letter opener, I'm dead before Eddie sticks him for real. I didn't have a chance. And now I do, but for what? Tell me, for what? If he pulls through, why don't you ask him that for me. What in God's name did he think he was doing!

"Every time I shut my eyes now, I see his face hanging over me. I don't know how I'm ever going to sleep without seeing those fucking nostrils.

"And the deal's off. Not officially yet. But we'll never revive it after what's happened, never. It's just too goddamn spooky. We're just a bunch of crazy Jews to them now. He really fouled the water with that one. You watch, no matter what else happens, I'm going to be stuck with that building forever. And that god-damned face, too."